# What t

MW01514339

"I...loved this story. It has a bit of everything. Romance, intrigue and action, there is something for everyone." - *Sime~Gen, Inc.*

"There aren't enough words to accurately describe how I felt about this novel. I wept, laughed, and fell in love. Crimson Rose is certainly not a novel to be missed. It holds a spot on my 'keeper' shelf." - *Sharyn McGinty, In the Library*

"The storyline is one that keeps you wanting to read to the finish. I have read many books that bring tears to my eyes but not many that have actually made me weep like this one did." - *Shirley Alguire, Sensual Romance Reviews*

"Crimson Rose is a touching tale of a woman who, despite the odds that life throws at her, still has an optimistic view of life. ... Crimson Rose will touch your heart and make you count your blessings. I think you will enjoy this book as much as I did." - *Barb Hicks, Road To Romance*

**CRIMSON ROSE**
An Ellora's Cave publication.

Ellora's Cave Publishing, Inc.
PO Box 787
Hudson, OH 44236-0787

ISBN # 1-84360-804-9
ISBN MS Reader (LIT) # 1-84360-168-0
ISBN Mobipocket (PRC) # 1-84360-169-9
Other available formats (no ISBNs are assigned):
Adobe (PDF), Rocketbook (RB), & HTML



Edited by *Christina Brashear, Martha Punches and Delyn Eagling*
Cover art by *R. Casteel.*

# CRIMSON ROSE

*R. CASTEEL*

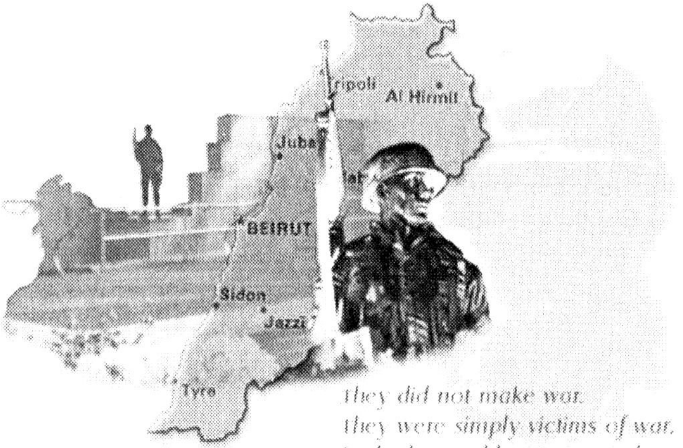


*They did not make war.*
*they were simply victims of war,*
*in the honorable attempt to keep*
*the peace. the gift of these men*
*was of the ultimate quality and*
*we know that it was of such value*
*that it cannot be given again.*

Crimson Rose is dedicated to the memory of those who gave their all, and to those whose lives were forever changed. May their sacrifice never be forgotten.

# ACKNOWLEDGEMENTS

I would like to thank the United States Marine Corps Public Affairs Office at Marine Corps Base Camp Lejeune, for their invaluable assistance in the writing of this book. While the characters of this book are of my own creation, the events concerning the bombing that occurred on October 23, 1983 are not.

I would also like to thank President Reagan's Library for providing the transcripts of his speeches relating to this tragedy in American history.

To Vanderbilt University for providing invaluable information from their archives of News transcripts.

A special thanks to the Beirut Memorial online for the use of the graphics. For more information about the memorial go to http://www.beirut-memorial.org.

Last but not least to the many friends who encouraged me in this endeavor without whose support, *The Crimson Rose* would not have been possible.

*R. CASTEEL*

US Navy (Ret.)

# Chapter One

Standing in the Jacksonville, North Carolina Courthouse, Rose Ann Shawnassy listened to the Justice-of-the Peace read the ceremony that was changing her name to Mrs. Mark Grady. Mark stood handsomely beside her in his spotless dress blue uniform of the United States Marine Corp, his new sergeant's chevron worn proudly on his sleeve. Five months ago, she hadn't even known he existed.

"I now pronounce you man and wife," intoned the Justice-of-the-Peace. "You may kiss the bride."

The kiss was hard and quick as one of Mark's fellow marines separated them. "You had that before the wedding. We're going to miss the bus. Let's go."

She placed her hand on her flat stomach. This shouldn't have happened. Thanks to a faulty condom, a missed period, and a trip to the doctor, she was Mrs. Rose Ann Grady.

Rose watched as her husband of less than a minute was propelled out the door at a dead run. She heard the car engine start and a squeal of tires as they headed back to Camp Lejeune to catch the bus to the airport.

She looked at her hand and the plain gold band that encircled her finger. They had bought the ring yesterday at one of the pawnshops on Court Street, commonly referred to as *The Strip*. A section of highway that was ablaze with neon lights advertising tattoos, cold beer, cheap rooms, and greasy food.

Running away from home and an alcoholic abusive father at age thirteen, she had lived on the streets. That's where retired Gunny Sergeant Sylvester O'Toul had found her cold, wet, and hungry, pillaging for food in the trash bin behind his restaurant.

His wife Maggie had cleaned her up, fed her, and given her a place to sleep. When they offered room and board in exchange for working as a waitress she agreed. There had been one condition. She had to finish her education.

Two days after she received her G.E.D., Maggie suffered a stroke. For days, Rose sat by her side taking care of her until a second stroke claimed her life. It had been up to Rose to pick up the pieces and handle the everyday business of the café.

After Maggie died, she had moved into the small apartment over the café that, for the last three years, she had called home.

Rose looked at the marriage license she held in her hand. It seemed strange that this piece of paper dated September 8, 1983 had changed anything. She didn't feel married; there would be no honeymoon. Mark was en route to Lebanon as one of the United Nations Peacekeeping Force in Beirut.

Outside, the morning sun was already baking the pavement. She hesitantly approached Mark's car. Even with the window down, the inside was hot as a blast furnace. She had only recently gotten her license and the black Firebird Mark kept polished to a mirror finish frightened her to death.

She started the engine. Although the muffler was new, it still couldn't hide the throaty raw power. Mark had beamed with pride when he talked about the engine being a SD455, how much horsepower it produced and the compression ratios. She wasn't quite sure what all that was. He had shown her how to check the oil and water, that's all she cared to know.

Placing the gearshift in the reverse position, she carefully let out the clutch and stepped on the gas pedal. The car jerked backwards with a squeal of tires. Slamming on the brakes, she killed the engine. She wiped the sweat from her face and restarted the engine. This time she didn't use any pressure on the accelerator and backed out of the parking space, changing gears as she eased into the street. "Please," she murmured. "Just let me get you back home in one piece."

Pulling behind the café, she breathed a silent prayer of thanks as she slipped into a parking spot. Rose pulled the large fitted cover from the trunk. Helping Mark do this, it had always seemed easy. Sweat ran down her face and neck as she worked to stretch the fabric over the Firebird. "There, safe and sound 'til Mark gets back." With a smile and a slap on the trunk lid, she went upstairs to change. Her wedding dress wasn't in the latest fashion, but unwilling to dip into her savings it was what she could afford. She hung up the dress in the back of her tiny closet, gently smoothing out a wrinkle. She didn't even have pictures of her wedding.

Rose brushed away the tear and donned her waitress uniform. Glancing at the clock, she noticed the time. Almost noon, the lunch hour had started and she was late.

Entering the café through the private entrance, she received an exasperated look from Debbie, the other waitress.

"Glad you're back." Debbie carried an order to a table. "This place has been a madhouse all morning."

She slipped an apron on. Later, she could feel sorry for herself over the hurry-up wedding and the lack of pictures. In her childhood dreams and fantasies, she had always wanted a fancy wedding with bridesmaids and a pretty wedding cake. In reality, she clung to what really mattered, that Mark did love her.

Reaching hurriedly through the service window for the next order, her hand became trapped. Looking through the narrow opening, she watched Gunny's face change from shock to anger and then hurt. She had forgotten to take off the wedding band.

"Get in here!"

The tears in his eyes balanced precariously on his lashes as he gently grasped her shoulders with both hands. She had seen Gunny cry twice in the four years she had live and worked there. When she received her diploma and when Maggie died.

"After all we have done for you. This is how you repay our kindness? By getting married to a man you've only known for five months? You didn't even allow me the honor of giving away the bride." The bell sounded in the window for another order bringing Sylvester back to the pressing business of his customers. Taking the ticket off the counter, he stared at it. "You pregnant?"

"Six weeks." Rose hung her head. If Gunny had yelled, cursed, or thrown something she could have handled it. His dropped shoulders and creased brow tore at her heart. "I'm sorry Gunny."

"What's done is done." He placed a finger beneath her chin and lifted her head. "We'll talk later." He gave her a kiss on the forehead and turned back to the steam table.

At two o'clock, Pete arrived to begin the evening meal. "Hi Rose." He waved from across the room. "Get your boyfriend off this morning in time to catch his bus?"

Rose smiled. "Hi Pete. Haven't heard from him since he left, so I guess he made it on time."

"That his car in back? I'm surprised he let you keep it. You promise him something he couldn't refuse for the privilege?" He strolled into the kitchen without waiting for a reply.

"She what?" Pete's startled voice was heard from the kitchen. He barreled through the swinging doors. "Tell ole Pete that the Gunny's pulling his leg. You didn't get married to a no-account marine. Didn't we warn you about these young bucks? Dammit girl!"

Rose held up her hand and displayed the gold band around her finger.

"Humph, I don't know whether to congratulate you or turn you over my knee."

Rose watched the scowl disappear as a smile began to form.

"Maybe it's best this way. Gunny and I would have fought to see who would walk you down the aisle." He gave Rose a big hug. "Congratulations dear. Of all the boys that come in here, I think you picked a good one."

"Thanks Pete," she whispered against his neck. "I appreciate that."

No sooner had Pete relinquished his hold, than Rose was crushed in another hug, this time from Debbie, the other daytime waitress. "You silly goose! Couldn't you even tell your best friend? Didn't we promise to be bridesmaids for each other?"

She gave Deb a hug in return. "I'm sorry; with Mark leaving today there just wasn't time to plan anything else. When he gets back in March we can plan a regular ceremony and these two old leathernecks can fight it out."

"I heard that!" a shout came from the kitchen.

The banter between them and the congratulations of a couple of customers relieved the tension that had been present since her earlier conversation with Gunny.

Gunny came out of the kitchen and poured a cup of coffee. He held up an empty cup to her. She gave him a thumbs-up and followed him to a booth.

"Rose, I couldn't care for you any more if you were my own daughter. Remember that rainy night four years ago, when we took you in. You were the daughter Maggie never had. You filled the emptiness in our lives. I think of you as family and you're all I have. I'm disappointed that you felt you couldn't come and talk to me about you and Mark. I know you two feel deeply about each other. Knew this would happen someday. Just wasn't figuring on waking up this morning, and finding that day was here."

"Tomorrow, we'll go to the base and get all the paper work started for your new life as the wife of a marine. I'll have Pete come in early so we can have the whole day."

That night, as Rose lay in bed, the cold ominous cloud of despair closed over her and sent her spirits crashing. The months of watching her mother die of cancer. The living in constant fear of an abusive father, even the year spent living on the street begging for food and being raped had not brought on this depth of loneliness.

She had always been self-sufficient, a whole unto herself. Mark had changed all that. With him somewhere over the Atlantic Ocean, she felt torn in two. She sobbed into her pillow, grieving for a wedding night that was not to be.

The next day after filling out countless forms at Personnel, Rose finally received her dependent's identification. At the hospital, there were registration forms and medical history forms. Then she was prodded, poked and stuck so many times she felt like one of Gunny's basted hams.

"Rose, I am Doctor Sheala Rosenthal. Please, feel free to call me Sheala. I will be your physician throughout your pregnancy. The test results show that you and the baby are doing fine, just make sure you take your vitamins. If you don't have any questions, I want to see you in a month for another checkup."

Rose went to the waiting room to find Gunny. "All done. We can go home now."

"Not yet. Still have Dental Department." He laughed at her puckered lips and drooped shoulders. "Cheer up Rose. This is the last one. Promise, Scout's honor." He held up three fingers.

The corner of her mouth turned up and a twinkle brightened her eyes.

"Gunny, when were you a Scout?"

He looked to the ceiling as if trying to recall the dates.

"I wasn't, but I wanted to be one. Come on let's get this over with."

"If you insist." Rose took Gunny's arm and they headed off to find Dental.

She was glad to get home, even if she did have to work the evening shift. Entering the dining area the phone rang. She grabbed her apron with one hand and the phone with the other. "Gunny's. How may I help you?"

"Hi, Mrs. Grady."

"Mark!" she squealed. "Where are you?"

"Sugar, I just arrived at the embassy in Beirut. I have a meeting with the major, so I can't talk long. Just wanted to let you know I arrived, and in case I didn't say so before, I love you Rose Grady."

"I love you too, Mark," she cooed. "I miss you already."

"Gotta go babe. I'll write and call as often as I can. Bye."

Rose hung up the phone and realized something was different. It was quiet, too quiet. With the number of vehicles out front, the continuous undercurrent of low voices and kitchen noises was missing. Turning around she was met with a thunderous explosion.

"Surprise!"

She stood there in shock. It was late afternoon and sitting in the restaurant were many of their regular customers and most of the business owners from the strip. A huge banner hung over the counter. 'Congratulations Mrs. Rose Grady!' In the center of the dining area, a large three-tiered wedding cake. Beside the cake, Gunny and Pete stood smiling like proud parents.

Often snubbed by the more traditional business owners in town who considered them as the other side of the tracks, the people on the strip were a close-knit group.

They all knew Rose as an attractive, honest and hardworking young woman who could be depended on to always have a smile and kind word for everyone who entered the restaurant. They had shared her pain and grief when Maggie died. Now they were there to share her happiness.

Rose was overwhelmed by it all. Their thoughtfulness, added to just talking with Mark caused joyfulness to bubble up like a shaken bottle of champagne. The party didn't last long. Most had businesses to run. The banner was left in place after the party as the girls carted away the remains of the cake and dirty dishes and prepared for the evening rush.

Gunny lost track of how many tickets were written incorrectly and how many orders were delivered to the wrong table. He noticed even the customers took the mistakes in good stride. The brilliant eyes, the glowing smile brought forgiveness and more than a few raised eyebrows. Gunny recognized the radiant look of a woman in love.

All evening and into the night Mark's words, "I love you" played over and over in her heart like the melody of an old love song.

* * * * *

"Morning, Rose. Sorry I couldn't be here for the party last week. Congratulations." Hank handed over the mail and drank his coffee.

"Thank you. Glad to see you're up and around again. If sleet and snow doesn't stop the mail..."

Rose stared at the envelope in awe. Mrs. Rose Grady, 10395 Court St. Jacksonville N.C. Her first personal letter and it had her married name on it. She received the standard junk mail from the IRS and bank statements but no one else wrote. Her father wouldn't waste money on an envelope and stamp when it could be put to better use buying booze. He didn't know where she was, and that's the way she wanted it. She picked up the envelope and noticed the postmark. US Embassy, Beirut Lebanon, 10 SEP 1983. Her heart raced as she looked at the return address. Sgt. Mark Grady, 24th MAU, F.P.O., NY, NY.

"Well, don't just stand there." Gunny was leaning against the counter, a steaming cup of coffee barely visible in his large hand. "Go ahead and open it." Gunny had to grin when he watch Rose carefully open the envelope, as if the envelope itself was special.

*My Dear Rose*

*I miss you so very much. The whole flight over I wished you could be sitting by my side. I wish things could have been different, but with the baby on the way I knew this was for the best. Now I don't have to worry cause you can receive medical attention at the base. By now, Gunny has already taken you for an ID and to the hospital. If he hasn't then he's no Marine Gunny Sgt.. Marines take care of their own.*

*Our barracks is located at the Airport in Beirut. You should see the maze of barricades around the building. It would take a tank to break through. Security is as tight as Fort Knox. I don't see what all the fuss is for. These people are so busy fighting themselves they haven't got time for us.*

*Ever since the last embassy bombing, things have been quiet here. Not so in the surrounding areas. If they were expecting anything, they would let us keep our weapons ready. Seems strange, that in a country where there is fighting and we are being shot at, we have to ask permission to lock and load.*

*Gotta go love, last call for mail to be sent.*

*Your loving husband,*

*Mark*

She read the letter a second time, memorizing the words.

"Well, what's he say," Gunny quizzed.

She handed Gunny the letter, barely keeping the excitement she felt from bubbling over.

Gunny read the letter and laughed. "It looks like you got yourself a good marine."

Her excitement overflowed. She grabbed Gunny's hands and danced around him, her shoulder length hair bouncing with each step. The door opened and a customer came in.

"Hi, Gunny, Rose," Bill waved. "The usual, please." Bill owned the Leathernecks Bar down the street. Every day around eleven a.m. he came in for his usual three eggs, double order of bacon, toast and coffee.

"Rose, married life must be good for you. I've never seen you look more beautiful. If my girls danced like that, my bar would be packed."

"Bill," she chided. "Your girls don't have to smile for your place to be full every night. It's not their face, the boys are looking at. Here's your coffee."

*September 20, 1983*

*Dearest Rose*

*Sorry for not writing sooner my love. Between standing duty at the barracks, the new embassy in west Beirut and the annex in east Beirut they have us riding around the countryside making our presence known. There is so much evidence of past conflicts here. Bombed out buildings scar the face of the country, thousands are homeless, the refugee camps are overcrowded. A person can feel the tension that is so prevalent in the area. In the Suf area southeast of Beirut, the Druze-Christian clashes are escalating in intensity*

*Even with the destruction, the country has beauty. The pointed towers of the Islamic mosques and the synagogues, many of which are in various stages of ruin. The majestic mountains with their snow capped peaks. The beautiful Mediterranean coastline that is fertile and rich. The interior of the country is mostly desert sand and barren rocky hills.*

*I wish things here were different so that you could be with me. The open courtyards and sidewalk cafes where we could sit and try the local cuisine and sample the wine. We could stroll barefoot in the sandy beaches of the Mediterranean Sea. You ought to see are the local markets, they're called souks.* *Vendors set up booths all along the street and alleys and sell handmade articles, jewelry and household items. I plan to bring home one of their beautiful hand made rugs when I get leave in March.*

*I haven't told my family that we're married. I want to be there with you by my side when I do. Knowing my Mother, she will want to have another ceremony with reception and everything else that goes with it. Knowing the way the Gunny feels about you I can imagine he was disappointed not to walk you down the aisle. Tell him to break out his dress blues and polish the brass. Gotta go.*

*Love*

*Mark*

Rose felt elated over Mark's letter, a real wedding with bridesmaids, friends, flowers, and pictures to treasure and show their grandchildren. A honeymoon in some intimate setting with a secluded beach where they could lay all day on the sand and make love under the stars. Warmth settled between her legs as she recalled their first time.

It had been over ninety degrees in her apartment. Mark was supposed to have duty that night so she stripped down to panties and bra. She opened the windows and door, hoping to capture any breeze that might find its way inside. Hearing a noise, she turned and saw Mark standing outside the screen.

She froze, unable to move as his stare roamed over her. She recognized the look in his eyes, the longing. Women would sit in the café and stare like that at a piece of chocolate éclair before ordering grapefruit or corn flakes. Her lips went dry. She moistened them with her tongue and saw Mark swallow hard.

He hesitated, his hand on the door. "May I come in?"

His voice was low, rough, as if it took great effort to speak. He was giving her the option. Something her attacker hadn't done. If she said, "No," she knew he would leave. If she said, "Wait 'til I get dressed," he would. The hunger Rose saw in his eyes burned within her. "Yes," a voice she barely recognized as her own invited.

The nightmare of her attack flooded her mind, the voices inside her head screamed at her to run but her feet were rooted to the floor, refusing to listen. By the time Mark stood in front of her, she was shaking.

"Are you sure about this?"

"Yes," she nodded. "No," her head shook. Then she wrapped her arms around him and sobbed. "Hold me Mark. Make the demons go away."

He lifted her in his arms and carried her to the couch. Breathing deeply, the fragrance of his aftershave filled her lungs. Her breast, pressed against his shirt, tingled and grew warm.

Her lips sought his mouth, when his tongue sought entrance and gently parted her lips she tensed remembering a foul breath of whisky.

Mark felt the change and gently held her. Closing his eyes, he tenderly kissed her forehead. "It's all right love. I didn't come here expecting this. You know that."

When Mark's lips touched hers again, Rose slammed the door on the demonic voices. Feeling his hardness against her hip, she had to have this. Now, tonight and with Mark. "Make love to me Mark," she whimpered.

"Slow down my wild Rose," he breathed. "We have all night and I need to go to the store for a minute before we continue."

"Why now?" She didn't want this to stop. "What's wrong?" She could feel the warmth of his breath on her face.

"Oh, God, Rose…I don't have anything with me."

She doubted that most men would stop at this point. Feeling the evidence of his need and marveling at his control, her heart swelled with emotion at his thoughtfulness. "There's a gas station on the corner." Her voice quivered with passion. "Hurry, before I change my mind."

He gave her a quick kiss, "If you do, I'll survive."

At the door, he turned and gave her a heated sultry glare and then he was gone. The voices inside her screamed at her to stop this but her body refused to listen. Her breast throbbed with anticipation and every nerve vibrated like a taunt violin string.

She met him at the door with a searching kiss when he returned.

"Haven't changed your mind?" he teased.

"No," She took his hand and led him to her bed.

"Do you, uh, want the light off?"

"I don't want darkness." Darkness brought back vivid memories of another time and place, a time when she had said no.

Mark sat beside her and touched her face. Her eyes were large and frightened. "I won't hurt you Rose, I could never do that."

Rose watched with open fascination as Mark undressed.

"I—I know." With trembling hands, she reached behind her, unclasped her bra, and let it fall to the floor. He hesitated, and reverently touched her.

"Mark," she whispered. "I've never done—this when..."

"I know," he kissed her. "We have all night." Taking the weight of one breast in his hand, Mark slowly caressed her nipple between thumb and finger and eased her back on the bed. Leaving a trail of kisses down her neck, he captured the nipple he had been teasing with his mouth.

The shear pleasure of it lifted her in an arch off the bed. A groan from deep within was torn from her. She felt his fingers tracing small circles in the hair between her legs. Wantonly Rose spread her legs to give him access. "Now—please," she begged.

Mark paused and turned away. Taking a foil packet from his pants he sheathed himself. Turning back to Rose he gently entered her warmth.

Rose smiled at the memory. That night the fears and nightmares had been laid to rest. Her attacker, although never caught, could no longer haunt her. She no longer feared him.

*September 28, 1983*

*Dearest Mark,*

*Received your letter yesterday. You were right about Gunny. He was hurt over not walking me down the aisle. He forgave me and took me to the base, grumbling the whole time. "Been retired for eleven years and still having to nursemaid wet-behind-the-ears marines."*

*I miss you. I read your letters every night and dream of being with you. I have a calendar where I am marking off the days 'til you get home. I ache for you at night and long to be in your arms again. You are the first thought I have in the morning and the last at night. I love you so much. I never knew life could be so wonderful. I used to go through each day surviving just for the next. Now I have you, the baby, and our future to hold on to.*

*I know with the bombings and fighting over there, you are kept busy. Call when you can, but if you can't, know that I love you.*

*Rose*

# Chapter Two

Before going downstairs, Rose marked off another day. She was one day closer. The little morning ritual with the calendar was a great morale booster. Humming a popular country love song, she entered the café though the private entrance, and gave Gunny a kiss on the cheek. "Morning."

"The rose has blossomed into a beautiful flower," he beamed proudly. "Pregnancy agrees with you. Now don't argue, I have heard several customers comment on how bright and cheerful you are lately, more so that normal. Actually I think the term used was radiant."

"Gunny, the only thing missing in my life right now is Mark beside me. It won't be long before he's home. I just hope he has time to call." She reached up and turned the TV on to the news. She'd never watched the news before. Never cared much what happened outside. Now she devoured the news for any information of the Middle East. Even in the midst of the hustle and bustle of a busy mealtime, she had one ear tuned to the TV. Comparing the letters from Mark and what she heard on the different stations, the American people were being shortchanged.

"Good Morning, This is your National News for October 9, 1983. In the early morning hours near the Airport in Beirut a surprise attack has left the first American casualties since the latest cease-fire began."

Rose's shuddered as she heard the report. The elation of the morning cooled and an icy sword of fear pierced her soul.

Gunny heard the report. Coming up to Rose, he put his arm around her shoulder. "Unfortunately this is part of it," he whispered. "I know this isn't easy, it never is, the waiting and the living with the fear. You're a strong woman; put your smile back on. Customers are waiting."

She swallowed the bile that had risen and lodged in her throat. Blinking away the tears, she gave him a weak attempt at a smile.

Gunny quirked his head and looked at her over the top of his glasses.

She forced a beaming smile she did not feel and with faltering steps carried the breakfast order out to the table. Somehow, she found the resolve from deep within to make it through the day. Without bothering to undress and shower she collapsed on her bed, dissolved into tears and cried herself to sleep.

The next morning as Hank dropped off the mail, Rose noticed the Embassy markings and excitedly tore open the envelope.

*October 3, 1983*

*Dearest Rose,*

*I don't know if you've seen the news. There was a mortar and rocket attack on the Lebanese Army today. The patrol I was with was involved for a short period. We are all okay; the jeep didn't fare as well.*

*They call this a cease-fire. The only ones ceasing fire is us. We might as well ride around with signs saying; Go ahead, won't shoot back. We were just in the wrong place at the wrong time. I don't want you to worry.*

*The Captain just hollered so I need to go.*

*Missing you*

*Mark*

"The top news headlines for today, October 16, 1983. The Multi National Peacekeeping Force in Beirut again came under fire from snipers. For a closer look at the continuing trouble in Lebanon, we go live to our reporter in Beirut."

"Tensions are running high this evening after an early morning sniper attack. Snipers believed to be hidden somewhere in this Shiite Moslem neighborhood opened fire on a routine patrol of U.S. marines killing the officer present. The marines returned fire. It is unknown at this time if any of the snipers were killed. A marine spokesman said they hope to be able to get back into the area tomorrow and retrieve the officer's body. Now back to our New York studio."

"Riots broke out between Moslems and Israeli troops in Nabatiyeh, Lebanon..."

Rose tuned out the rest of the broadcast and focused on pouring a cup of coffee. She was torn between hearing the news, which sometimes gripped her heart like an iron fist, and turning off the TV. Not hearing, not knowing was worse.

The lunch crowd had cleared out and Rose looked at the clock. "Gunny," she yelled. "I'm leaving for my Doctor's appointment."

He waved, and went back to filling the large dishwasher.

Stripping off the cloth cover on Mark's Firebird she climbed in and headed for the base. She was beginning to get the feel of all the power under the hood. At least she didn't chirp the tires every time she gave it gas.

Stepping from the car, Rose noticed another woman, huge from pregnancy, waddling across the parking lot toward the hospital. One hand was flat across her back; the other was cradled under her extended stomach. Catching up to her, Rose slowed her steps. "Do you need any help?"

She smiled. "Only if you can bring the bathroom out here. Excuse me, we're on base now, it's called the Head. Must be a 'man thing' to call a place where you pee the *Head.*"

Rose laughed. "How soon are you due?"

"Oh God, not soon enough. They tell me next week. I'm ready now, but junior is taking his time. I'm Linda; my husband is with the Twenty-fourth MAU in Beirut."

"I'm Rose, me too. I mean my husband is there too. He left here on September 8."

Linda looked at Rose's flat waist line with envy. "Are you expecting?"

"Yes, I'm almost twelve weeks," Rose beamed.

"I remember those days," Linda recalled. "They seem like a million years ago."

Rose opened the door for Linda and watched as she waddled down the hall looking for the Women's Head. *When Mark gets home I'll be that big. Will he still love and want me?*

As Rose sat in the waiting room she looked around at the other women there. *I wonder how many of their husbands are overseas.*

"Mrs. Grady, the doctor will see you now. Please change into this gown and lie down on the table. The Doc will be right with you." The female navy corpsman closed the door.

Rose changed and waited. Half an hour later Doctor Rosenthal entered the room.

"Sorry to keep you waiting Rose. How have you been doing, any morning sickness?

"No, just a little nausea when around I'm greasy food," she laughed. "And working at Gunny's..." she shrugged.

"I've eaten there." Smiling at the unfinished sentence Sheala readied the ultrasound. "Let's see how you are progressing." She bared Rose's abdomen and applied the ultrasound gel.

Watching the monitor Sheala smiled. "Congratulations Rose, we have a heart beat."

Rose was elated. Tears of joy filled her eyes. "I wish Mark could see."

Sheala recognized the longing, the loneliness. She saw it every day. What good was it to be a Doctor and a Lt. Commander if she couldn't cut some red tape and pull strings every now and then? "You can get dressed Rose. But don't leave yet." She went to get her scissors.

Rose wondered what was taking so long.

Sheala opened the door. "Rose, would you please come with me?"

Rose followed the Doc down the hall way to an office. "There's a phone call for you Rose."

Picking up the phone, she was momentarily speechless as she heard Mark's voice. "Mark? Love, it's really you! How? I mean..."

"I miss you too love. I was called to the office, said it was urgent. Not that I mind, but personal calls on this line are rare. Someone pulled a lot of weight on this one."

Rose turned and watched as the door closed behind her. "Does a Navy doctor have enough weight?"

"What are the collar devices the doc is wearing?"

"Silver, oak leaves I think they're called." Remembering conversions she had heard around the café.

"Yep. That's enough weight," Mark replied. "What's up? Are you okay?"

"I'm fine. I got to hear the baby's heartbeat." Her voice broke. "I miss you so much Mark. I'm marking the calendar, counting the days 'til you're home."

"I've got a calendar too. I mark mine off every evening just before lights out."

"I do mine the first thing the next morning. It gives me a good feeling all day long that another one is gone."

Mark did a quick time calculation in his head. "You go down to work at five am, right?"

"Every morning but Sunday and Monday. Sunday is seven o'clock and Monday I'm off. Why?"

"If I mark my days off the calendar at Noon our time, then we will both be crossing them off at the same time."

"That would be great." Her voice took on a husky resonance. "I wish we could do something else together."

"Ah, my little green eyes, me too." He lowered his voice. "I don't know if this line is monitored or not. We better cool it. I might have a *hard* time explaining something to the major.

"I really don't care if someone is listening," said Rose. "I miss you making love to me, and if that offends someone listening then that's their tuff-titty. You can just bring your hard time home and I will take care of it for you."

Mark laughed 'til his side hurt. "Being pregnant sure brings out the wild side of my sweet Rose. Think I'll have to keep you that way."

"After seeing another marine's wife this morning, I'll have to veto that. She is ready to deliver any day now. Her husband is in Beirut too."

"You have to be talking about Linda. That's all Jason can talk about. If he's this bad now, I'm putting in for a transfer after the baby is born. Then again, I'll probably be worse when ours has popped out into this world."

"Mark, before we take advantage of this call and get the Doc in trouble I'd better go. I love you. Please take care; my world would end if something happened to you."

"Love, I'll be fine. Don't wash the gold dust off your pretty eyes. I have a wonderful, lovely and pregnant wife waiting for me."

"Bye Mark," she whispered. "I love you." She hung up the phone and went in search of Dr. Rosenthal.

"Excuse me..." Rose couldn't finish. She wrapped her arms around Sheala, surprising the corpsman that was standing there. "Thank you...doesn't seem appropriate enough for what you did." She gave her a hug.

Sheala had tears in her own eyes and returned the embrace. "It was my pleasure Rose. Now go home and rest. Tell Gunny, I said not to work you so hard."

* * * * *

Rose stood in front of the calendar, waiting. At five o'clock, she took her magic marker and lined through the previous day. She grabbed a glass of juice and a slice of dry toast to settle her nausea and went downstairs. The smell of frying sausage and bacon hit her as she opened the door. This time, the toast didn't help. She barely made it to the bathroom.

Debbie handed her a cup of warm tea when she came out. "This always helped my sis. You've lasted longer than she ever did. She has four and with every one of them she started heaving after the first week."

"Thanks Deb, I'll try to remember how lucky I am the next time I'm on my knees in front of the porcelain throne."

"Don't mention it." She gave a flip of the hand. "What are friends for?"

Rose turned the TV on and prepared for the café to open at five-thirty.

She was taking an order for biscuits and gravy as the news turned to the Middle East.

"Skirmishes between Druse and Shiite Moslems today have placed the peace negotiations between Lebanon's warring factions in serious doubt. The National Salvation Front is rejecting the planned location for the reconciliation negotiations. Walid Jumblatt, leader of the Druse faction claims this site is unsafe. It is reported that Jumblatt's own militia is said to be contributing to the lack of safety in the region.

"In Beirut, following in the footsteps of continuing sniper attacks, a car bombing in the downtown area wounded several marines who were driving by at the time.

"The goal of the up coming negotiations..."

Debbie came over and gently touched Rose on the shoulder. "I think you grabbed the wrong table. Remember, we switched."

In a fog, Rose walked back to the counter.

Gunny came out from the kitchen. "Wounded is not dead," he whispered.

Taking a deep breath, she sighed. "Yeah, I know."

* * * * *

The alarm clock sounded and Rose swatted at it as if it were a mosquito. This was Sunday morning. Then she remembered the calendar. Climbing out of bed, she padded barefoot across the floor and marked off October 22. She was glad that one was gone. Last night had been rough. The café had been so busy she had gone down to help. They finally had to ask the last group of customers to leave an hour after regular closing. Not having the energy to even shower, she had stripped off her clothes and climbed into bed.

Rose had two hours before she had to go downstairs. She was going to make the most of it. Filling the tub with hot water, she dumped in a cap of lavender scented bath oil. Easing her tired body into the steaming fragrant water, she sighed with contentment. Closing her eyes, she allowed the soothing comfort of the lavender to gently pull her into dreamland.

*Mark was there, reaching out to her, but not quite making contact with her. No matter how hard she tried, she couldn't reach him. He was saying something to her. She couldn't hear his voice. Slowly she made out the words formed by his lips.*

*Remember I Love You.*

The strange dream and the cooling water woke her. She patted herself dry with a large terry cloth towel. It was seven o'clock.

Rose entered the café, thanks to falling asleep in the tub, she was late.

Their Sunday morning crowd was unexpectedly large. Deb was looking flustered already. Grabbing her apron she headed for the counter to deliver an order. It was several minutes before she took the time to hit the on button for the TV. A lady with dirt on her hands was telling about planting flowers and what type of soil was best to use.

Rose took another order, and headed over to clean a vacated table.

"We interrupt the regular scheduled broadcast to bring you this special report from the National Network News Room."

Carrying the tray to the kitchen, she was halted in her tracks.

"Just before six thirty AM local time, terrorists bombed the marine barracks in Beirut, Lebanon. For live coverage we go to the Beirut Airport, outside the marine headquarters."

"As you can see behind me, the devastation to the marine barracks is complete. Most of the marines, sailors, and soldiers staying here were still in their beds sleeping on this quiet Sunday morning. The death toll is expected to be high. Some I have talked to in the midst of the chaos say it could go higher than two hundred..."

The café had grown deathly quiet. Every eye was tuned to the set as the report continued. Rose watched in horror as the camera shot a close up of Mark's barracks. All that was left was a pile of rubble; smoke billowed across what used to be a parking lot.

Everything disappeared from view until all she could see was the picture in front of her. She became aware of hysterical screaming, not realizing it was her own. The dishes she held crashed to the floor. The screen faded, screaming stopped, as Rose fainted and fell amidst the broken dishes.

Debbie was across the room when the News Alert flashed across the screen. Cutting around tables and bumping customers who were staring in disbelief at the screen she raced to Rose's side. Everything moved in slow motion. She couldn't get her feet to move any faster. Deb watched the container of dishes and flatware crash to the floor. Reaching for Rose, she was unable to stop her from falling to the floor. Deb dropped beside Rose's still form; blood was already visible on the floor, flowing from between her legs.

"Oh God. No." she cried. "Gunny, call the ambulance." There was too much blood flowing to be a miscarriage as she had first thought. Gently feeling underneath Rose she ignored the cuts from the broken glass she received. Her hand touched the wooden handle of the knife. Debbie's heart sank. It was completely buried in Rose's leg. She held the knife in place, putting pressure on the wound as best she could.

"The ambulance is on the way." Gunny knelt beside her. "Keep pressure on the wound. I don't think we should move her. Are there any other cuts?"

"I don't know. I don't think so. I wasn't able to check everywhere." She looked at Gunny, begging for help. "Check and see, I can't let go."

He gently checked Rose's arms, removing the broken glass from beneath them. "Nothing serious, some minor cuts. No major bleeding here."

The sound of a siren cut through the stillness that had enveloped the café. Everyone waited in silence as the drama unfolded. A few could be seen on this Sunday morning doing something rarely done in Gunny's. They were praying, for the victims of the bombing and their families, many of whom they knew personally or through their place of business. They were praying for Rose, young, expecting, and most probably a widow less than two months after she married.

The ambulance crew arrived and with Gunny's help lifted Rose off the bed of broken glass; the apron had saved her from being cut any worse. They secured the imbedded knife with tape and applied a pressure bandage. Rose began to come around as they loaded her on the gurney.

Pete came flying into the parking lot, tires screamed in protest as he jammed on the brakes. "I saw the ambulance leave. Was it Rose?"

The two ex-marines hugged in the parking lot. "Go to the hospital," Pete ordered. "I'll take care of things here."

Gunny and Debbie left for the hospital, Pete went into the diner and stared at the TV. He watched the smoke, drifting across the parking lot, obscure the rescue efforts. The walking wounded, many with blood soaked bandages, sat in a makeshift triage area waiting to be taken for further medical treatment. The body count had already started as the camera panned along a row of bodies that were covered. Pete's own nightmares of war and death came flooding back.

Fighting back the rage at the tragic loss of lives, which were there simply to keep the peace, he turned to the customers. "The café is now closed. Rose is like a daughter to Gunny and me. My place is at the hospital."

One of the ladies stood and started clearing away her table. As if through some telepathic signal, every woman in the café started clearing the tables. Arms laden with dirty dishes, they entered Gunny and Pete's hallowed domain through swinging doors.

Roxanne, one of the topless dancers at the Leathernecks Bar, scolded Pete. "You just get yourself over to the hospital. I've done other things to support myself besides dancing for a bunch of horny sailors and marines. I know my way around the inside of a kitchen, and don't try any of that macho, jarhead bullheadedness with me. I'm not one of your, *once a marine always a marine, yes-sir boys. I'm a woman!"*

Pete knew how to retreat when faced with a superior defense. "Lock up when you leave." Pete paused in the doorway, "Roxy, thanks." He placed a hastily written sign in the window.

'Due to the Bombing in Beirut, Gunny's is CLOSED'.

* * * * *

They were watching the special coverage as Pete walked into the hospital emergency waiting room. Pete caught Gunny's eye and shake of the head. He sat down next to Debbie for the wait.

# Chapter Three

All eyes in the hospital waiting room were watching the horror of the bombing when the screen switched to the White House.

"President Reagan has just returned to the White House. For the last several hours, he has been conferring with his top advisors concerning this mornings bombing in Beirut, Lebanon. We are live at the South Portico of the White House where the President of the United States is about to speak."

"I'm not going to take any questions this morning because we're going right into meetings on the events that have taken place on this tragic weekend. But I would like to make this statement:

"I know there are no words that can express our sorrow and grief over the loss of those splendid young men and the injury to so many others. I know there are no words, also, that can ease the burden of grief for the families of those young men.

"Likewise, there are no words to properly express our outrage and, I think, the outrage of all Americans at the despicable act, following as it does on the one perpetrated several months ago, in the spring, that took the lives of scores of people at our Embassy in that same city, in Beirut.

"But I think we should all recognize that these deeds make so evident the bestial nature of those who would assume power if they could have their way and drive us out of that area that we must be more determined than ever that they cannot take over that vital and strategic area of the Earth or, for that matter, any other part of the Earth.

"Thank you."

"Time we kicked some ass," Pete swore.

"That place would be another Vietnam." Gunny protested. "Whose would you start kicking first? There are so many different factions fighting. You have your Greek Orthodox, Roman Catholic, Protestant, and Armenian on one hand. On the other, you've got the Sunnis, Shiites, Maronite, and Druze. Then you can throw in several thousand pissed off Palestinians and a handful of terrorists from other countries."

"All right, enough." Pete held up his hands in defense. "Jeeezz, sorry I said anything."

"Party waiting for Rose Grady," a corpsman announced.

All three stood.

"Mrs. Grady is fine, thanks to your quick help," he praised them. "They have taken her to room 412B. You can go on up."

"How's the baby?" Gunny fearfully asked.

The Corpsman flashed him a smile. "The baby's fine."

They all breathed a sigh of relief and headed to the fourth floor.

Rose greeted them with a shaky smile. "Who's minding the store?"

"It's closed for the day." Gunny quietly stated.

"Sorry I caused…all the problems." Her voice broke as tears hovered, threatening to flow down her cheeks.

Gunny placed a hand on her shoulder and Rose dissolved into tears. "I know Mark is dead. I can feel it inside."

"We don't know that for sure," Debbie tried to encourage.

"I do," she flatly stated.

Gunny looked into tear-filled gold speckled emerald eyes. In all his fifty-five years, he couldn't recall seeing anyone's eyes with that exact coloring. He also read with certainty that Rose could not be persuaded to wait for conformation from the marines. A hysterical woman would not meet the arrival of the envoy from the Marine Liaison office.

"There's not a single reason for you all to hang around here. Go home," she ordered. "I'm fine. The doctors said I could go home tomorrow."

Rose gave the three friends a warm smile she didn't feel like giving and waved as they left. Right now, all she wanted was to have some time to be alone. She stared out the window; the flag was already at half-mast. That was the only sign that something was different. Even that would go back to normal in a few days.

Lt Commander Sheala Rosenthal knocked lightly on the doorsill. "Hi Rose, just wanted to stop by and see how you're doing."

"I'm not really sure, might as well be honest. I want to thank you again for the arranging the call to Mark the other day." She wiped at the tears again threatening to flow.

Sheala sat down on the bed and smoothed Rose's hair. "Rose, you don't know Mark is dead. No one knows who was killed or injured."

"I know," there was finality in those two words.

"How do you know, Rose," inquiring softly.

"I know this is going to sound weird," She stared into Sheala's eyes. "I saw him this morning, in a dream."

"In a dream," Sheala repeated. "Rose, you've had a shock. What you need right now is to get some rest." She turned to leave. "By the way, Linda, the young woman you were talking to the other day. She gave birth last night to a healthy baby boy."

When Sheala left, Rose placed her hand protectively over the life that was growing inside her. Linda had her baby. "Even in death—life goes on," she whispered to an empty room.

She turned the TV on.

"In the aftermath of the bombing this morning, President Reagan is committed to keeping a full marine contingent in the region. Defense Secretary Casper Weinberger agrees, feeling that the size of the force in place in Beirut is appropriate for their mission…The White House is said to be blaming terrorists linked to Ayatollah Khomeini's regime."

"Elsewhere in Washington…Representative Samuel Stratton along with Senators Ernest Hollings, Sam Nunn, Charles Mathias, John Glenn and Howard Baker are calling for the immediate withdrawal of marines….

"Even as families sit and wait fearfully for information of their loved ones more marines are preparing to leave for Beirut from Camp Lejeune…"

She turned her head to the window, drifting off to sleep as silent tears of grief soaked her pillow.

The next morning right after breakfast there was a knock on the door. Two marines in dress blues were standing in the hall.

"Come in," she invited. "I've been expecting you."

"Excuse me?"

The captain's expression was almost comical.

"You have come to inform me of my husband's death in Beirut."

"With the utmost sincere sympathy of the Marine Corps Mrs. Grady," he cleared his voice. "Yes, we regrettably have come for that reason. There will be a memorial service here at the base. You will be informed of the date and time. Mrs. Grady, the marines look after their own." He handed her a card. "If you need anything, day or night, call this number. It's a family support group on the base, made up of volunteers who have gone through this tragedy themselves. One of them will be by to visit you. It may be a few days."

"Thank you for coming," she paused. "Can you tell me if Linda's husband is dead? Their baby was born last night."

"We just left her room," the other marine informed her.

"Thank you." Without waiting for them to leave, Rose climbed out of bed and stepped into her slippers. While she was putting on the robe, a navy corpsman was walking by and saw her.

"Just where do you think you're going," he inquired rather harshly. "You are supposed to have help. That was a serious injury you suffered."

"I am going to the maternity ward," she declared. "If you want to help then you can get a wheelchair. If not then stand aside. I can walk on my own."

"You can't do that!" his tone sharp.

"Watch me." Rose started to carefully walk to the door.

"I'll get a chair." Reluctantly giving in, he returned a moment later pushing a wheel chair. "You know I could get in trouble for this."

"Which would be worse?" she questioned. "Giving me a chair or allowing me to walk up there?"

"Get in." He pushed her out the door and down the hall.

Linda was sobbing, curled into a fetal position in the center of the bed. Rose took over command of the chair and wheeled herself into the room. Carefully getting out of the chair, she sat on the bed.

"Linda," she called softly.

She looked up and seeing who it was, reached for Rose.

"The liaison lieutenant told me. I'm so sorry."

"Not you too, Rose, there's so many. I just heard on the news the death toll has gone over two hundred. How could this happen Rose? How?" A fresh wave of sobs racked her body. "Jason will never know his son. It's so unfair."

They held each other and cried tears of grief, frustration, and anger at their world that had suddenly been turned upside down.

* * * * *

"For National Network News this is the World Report. The top story in the nation and around the world is yesterday's bombing of the marine barracks in Beirut. Not since the Korean and Vietnam War's have we seen this many casualties. For a more in-depth report, we go live, to our reporter in Beirut."

"There has been talk here that a Lebanese Army colonel warned marines on several occasions of the possibility of just such an attack as did take place here yesterday. Marine Colonel Timothy Geraghty feels that all reasonable precautions against terrorist assaults were taken.

"The wounded of yesterdays bombing are being evacuated to West Germany, Italy, and Cyprus. Marine replacements already en route to Beirut are in West Germany on a stopover before continuing on to Beirut.

"Now we take you to our Washington DC correspondent."

"US intelligence has gathered information pointing to a possible Iranian connection to yesterday's bombing of marine compound in Beirut. They believe the bombing was masterminded by, a Moslem fanatic loyal to Ayatollah Khomeini. There have been questions raised, in light of this information, about the apparent lax security around marines in Beirut. Marine Commandant Paul Kelley is en route to Beirut to view first hand the devastation caused by Sunday's attack. For further developments we take you to Camp Lejeune, North Carolina."

"I'm outside the entrance to the marine base at Camp Lejeune, North Carolina. Many of the marines killed and wounded in yesterday's bombing were stationed here. As family members anxiously await word on the fate of their relatives, the city of Jacksonville is closing ranks around the base in support and help for the family members."

* * * * *

Ex-Special Forces Staff Sergeant William Dennis Grady sat at his parent's home impatiently waiting for a phone call or a visit from the U.S. Marine Liaison Office telling him the status of his brother. He was tired, having spent most of the night in the Nashville General Hospital with his mother. It had given Dad a chance for a few hours sleep. Something neither of them had received much of since his mother had collapsed yesterday upon hearing of the bombing. He turned the TV on again for the fifth time. Why hadn't someone called? They were supposedly contacting the families. Yet, he had heard nothing. He pounded his fist on the arm of the couch. "Damn."

About to turn the TV off again he noticed the toll free number that family members could call. Grabbing the phone, he hurriedly dialed the number.

"This is the marine hot line, are you a family member."

Dennis took a deep breath and thought, *Lady, why else would I be calling this number?*

"Yes. I'm his brother."

"Name and rank of the service member you are inquiring about please?"

"Sergeant Mark Grady, I'm his brother William Dennis Grady."

"I am sorry Mr. Grady, your brother is on the casualty list. On behalf of the U.S. Marine Corps and the United States Government, we offer our sympathy."

"I want to know why we weren't informed earlier of this. I am a veteran, Special Forces." The buildup of the past hours frustrations were coming out but Dennis didn't care. "Isn't it still standard practice to send a liaison to the next of kin and inform them in person."

"We already have sir. First thing this morning."

"No one has been here this morning." His voice grew deadly calm as years of military training took over. "Who did you notify, if I might ask."

"Certainly can. We notified Mrs. Rose Grady, his wife."

Dennis couldn't believe what he'd just heard. "I'm sorry you must have the wrong person. Mark Grady didn't have a wife."

"There is only one Sgt. Mark Grady listed as being stationed in Beirut. Rose Grady of Jacksonville, North Carolina is listed as next of kin. That's all the information I have. I'm sorry I can't be of more help. I'll give you the number on base that has been set up to help family members."

Dennis wrote down the number and called.

"Camp Lejeune, this is Captain Fredrick of the Liaison Office."

"This is Dennis Grady, in Nashville, Tennessee. I called the hotline number and they gave me this number. Seems there has been a mix-up somewhere. They told me my brother Sgt. Mark Grady of the twenty-fourth MAU had a Rose Grady listed as next of kin. My brother wasn't married."

"I'm sorry Mr. Grady. There has been no mix-up. I personally talked to Mrs. Grady this morning at the base hospital."

"Can you tell me when my brother supposedly got married?" This was crazy.

"I'm sorry but I don't have that information," Fredrick apologized. "Even if I did have it, I couldn't give the information over the phone."

"Thank you for your help." Dennis hung up the phone with force.

Later, he would get to the bottom of this mess. If he couldn't, he had no business running the Operations Department of Grady Security and Investigations in Nashville. Right now, it was his job to tell his parents their son was dead.

* * * * *

Dennis's plane touched down in Jacksonville just after eight o'clock that night. Wanting to be close to the base, he rented a car and located a motel on the strip. It looked like it was frequented by customers that paid by the hour, instead of the day.

"Where's a place close by to get a decent meal this time of night?" Dennis asked the night clerk.

"Closest is Gunny's, just down the strip about half a mile. Good food and a decent price, course you not being a marine they might charge you double," he said jokingly. "You're lucky you found a room around here. Everything is filling up fast, family members calling in from all over reserving rooms for the memorial service. President Reagan is even going to be here. In another day or two there won't be a room this side of Jacksonville to be found."

"Thanks." Dennis pocketed the room key and headed for Gunny's. The drive brought back memories of his days in the military. They might have different names but the strip was still the same in every military town. The pawnshops, tattoo parlors, the topless bars, and rundown motels. Throw in a few fast food restaurants, gas stations, and Laundromats and you have an area that attracts servicemen like ants to a picnic. Gunny's would be run by a retired Gunny Sergeant; there would be pictures of buddies he had served with, probably from Vietnam. If you could get him talking he could fill you head with horror stories that would make a normal man afraid to sleep for a week.

Dennis saw the sign and pulled in. Walking through the door, the cafe was just as he figured. He sat at a booth and looked at the pictures on the wall. Behind every picture was a story. Some of which could never be told. He had a few of his own that were locked away. Special orders that for the Special Forces, never officially existed. If a casualty occurred it was a training mission accident. He was sick of the lies and cover-ups in the name of national security.

A tired looking waitress came over to take his order. "Long day," he inquired.

"Double shift," she returned. "One of the girls is in the hospital. They decided to keep her one more day."

"Nothing serious I hope?" He asked making conversation.

"Rose fainted and fell on a knife Sunday morning." She pulled out her pad. "You ready to order?"

"Rose?" His pulse picked up at the name. Outwardly, he appeared disinterested.

"Yeah, Rose Grady, she's been here about four years now. She lives upstairs over the café. Gunny found her on the street, took her in, and gave her a job. Almost like a daughter to him. Anyway, she was working Sunday morning when the news came in about the bombing in Beirut. Her husband was stationed over there. She fainted and fell on a knife."

Dennis gave his order and the waitress left. He couldn't believe his stroke of luck. Of all the places in town, he ended up at the place where this woman who called herself Mrs. Grady worked. Half the work he needed to do was already done. Thanks to an over-talkative waitress.

After he finished his meal, Dennis headed back to get some sleep. Tomorrow was going to be a busy day.

* * * * *

"Pete, what a pleasant surprise," Rose greeted. "What brings you here this early."

"Gunny and I picked straws to see who would cook or come to get your lazy backside back home and I lost," he joked. "Gunny is still trying to find everything after Roxanne cleaned up Sunday."

Rose scowled and fidgeted in the bed. "They just started the red tape to get me out of here. Don't know how long it will be. You might as well go have a cup of your coffee downstairs."

"My coffee?" Pete feigned a hurt expression. "You badmouthing my coffee again.

"Let's just say I figured out why you wanted the night shift at the Café. You come in here every morning and make their coffee." She laughed as Pete dramatically placed his hands over his heart.

"My darling Rose, you wound me."

"Pete, don't quit your night job. You can't make coffee, or act, but you're a good cook."

"Took me twenty years to perfect my coffee, it just…"

"Proves that you don't appreciate the finer things in life 'til you're older," she finished for him. "Get out of here so I can get dressed. You did bring me some clothes?"

Pete handed her a bag. "I'll find out how long it will be and come back for you."

* * * * *

Dennis walked into the courthouse and found the record's department.

"May I help you?" inquired a woman behind the counter.

"I am looking for a copy of my brother's marriage license." The way to make a lie believable was to sprinkle it with just enough truth, and keep it simple. "Mark went on his honeymoon and somehow lost it. He asked me to stop by and get a copy for him."

"What's his name?" she asked.

"Mark Grady, I'm Dennis, his wife's name is Rose.

She checked her records. "Here it is, married September 8, 1983, Jacksonville, NC. That will be three dollars for the copy."

Dennis paid her and stuck the copy in his pocket. "Thank you for your help."

He stepped outside and read the license. "Ceremony Performed by The Honorable Walt Mathis, Justice-of-the-Peace." Dennis found the judge's office and knocked on the door.

The judge listened to Dennis. "Yes, I remember the couple. He was in his dress uniform had two friends with him. The groom hardly got a decent kiss before he was whisked out of here. Left his new bride at the altar holding a set of keys in her hand."

"So the marriage isn't legal unless it is consummated, right?" Dennis questioned.

"I have a feeling that with the hurry they were in, that part had already taken place." The judge smiled knowingly.

"Thank you for your time, sir." They shook hands and Dennis left. *The little gold digging hussy.* He muttered an oath that brought a startled gasp from an elderly lady in the hall.

Dennis headed back to the hotel. Time to check in at home. Stretching his six-foot frame out on the bed, he reached for the phone and dialed, waiting as the phone rang at home.

"Dad, how's Mother?"

"I'm relieved she's feeling better. I got lucky on this end. Found the woman. She works in a greasy spoon outside the base."

"Yeah, the marriage is real, I talked to the judge that performed the ceremony. According to him, Mark ran to catch the plane for Beirut leaving her at the altar. I haven't actually met her. I don't plan on telling her who I am, when I do."

"The whole thing smells to me. I mean why wouldn't Mark say something in his letters. Not that there were very many. Why keep the thing secret."

"I agree Dad, totally out of character."

"No," warned Dennis. "I don't think we should try to fight it right now. It would bring too much publicity. Grieving widow of American serviceman hounded by the fallen hero's family."

"That's the way I figured. Do a quiet investigation and stay in the background. See which way she goes after she meets you and Mother."

"I agree, I don't think she knows about us or she would have tried to contact us since the wedding."

"Haven't found anything yet Dad, except that she was a throwaway. The owner of the café took her in off the street. They could be working a scam on unsuspecting marines."

"You don't want to stay at this hotel."

Dennis laughed, "Yeah! It's that kinda place."

"I'll get you and Mother a room in a Holiday Inn or Howard's."

"I'll call you back once I've met her. She's in the hospital. I was told she fainted at the news, and fell on a knife."

"No nothing else."

"I'll keep in touch. Bye"

Dennis looked up a number and dialed.

"Yes, I'd like to book a room please for the third through the sixth next week."

"Two occupants please."

Dennis gave the desk clerk his card number and hung up. Time to do some more checking on dear brother's bride.

# Chapter Four

A few minutes later, he was parked at Gunny's. There were very few vehicles in the lot. The same waitress was on duty.

"Back again?" She asked as she brought a cup of coffee over.

"I could say the same about you."

"Regular shift today." She moved her head in the direction of the other girl. "She has the double shift. What can I get you?"

"Too late for breakfast?" he inquired.

"Heavens sake no!" she laughed. "We serve that around here all day long."

"Good, I'm starved." Picking up the menu, he gave it a quick glance. "I'll have the short stack, two eggs well, and an order of sausage."

Dennis had taken a booth at the back of the little café giving him an unobstructed view of the room. This was the hardest part of investigation work, the waiting and watching, the boredom. A car pulled up and a heavyset man got out and came in.

'Hi Debbie, Gunny." He waved to Gunny, visible through the server slot. "How's Rose doing? Is she coming home today?"

*Regular*, Dennis thought, *didn't order, has the same thing every morning.*

"Pete is picking her up." She poured the coffee. "There they are now."

Dennis felt his nerves tingle. Inside his body was like a coiled spring. To others, he knew he showed the typical interest of a stranger. He barely glanced at the window.

Dennis watched as two people walked in, he quickly dismissed the older man. Shifting his eyes away from the morning paper, he focused his attention on the young woman. She was young, medium build, and attractive with some nice curves. What stood out was the crimson hair. It resembled a halo of fire around her face. She walked slowly, favoring her right leg. The waitresses beamed and gathered around her, welcoming her back. The cook came out and gave her a big hug. The café was large enough that he only caught bits and pieces of the conversion.

So, this was Mark's wife. The cook was Gunny. "How charming," he muttered. His waitress asked Rose something in a low voice. He couldn't hear. *Just as I suspected.* He thought when Rose placed her hand low on her stomach. *She's claiming to be pregnant. If she is, I bet it isn't Mark's. He wouldn't make a mistake like that.* Gunny said something that she didn't agree with, he caught the "No," and a shake of her head that sent the shoulder length hair bouncing.

"I'm not going upstairs Gunny," she repeated. "I've been in a bed for two days now. I'll sit here at the cash register. The Doctor said, 'No lifting.' Now go back to the kitchen. Please."

Gunny threw his hands in the air and grumbling under his breath, went back through the swinging doors.

The waitress delivered his food and refilled his cup.

Dennis ate slowly. He was in no hurry to leave.

"Rose, it's good to see you again," greeted Bill. "Sorry to hear about your husband. Such a tragic loss of life." He took a hand in both of his. "If there is anything we can do, just ask."

"Thanks Bill." She leaned over and gave him a hug and a kiss on the cheek. "I appreciate that. Roxanne has already been a big help. Tell her thank you for me, please."

Rose glanced around the café. She didn't recognize the man in the back. His hair was the color of wet sand upon the beach, broad shoulders filled the blue shirt he wore. She thought he had been watching her, but it was probably her imagination. Just then, the door opened and the noon trade started coming in. She turned and greeted the customers.

"Anything else I can get for you?" his waitress asked. "More coffee?"

"Please." He pushed the cup closer to the edge of the table. "She seems so young to be a widow."

"Rose is eighteen." She filled the cup. "Age has nothing to do with being a widow."

"How long had they been married?" he asked.

"Not long." She glanced around at her tables.

"It's a shame, well I won't keep you. Thanks." He held up his cup. *I can't stall much longer.* The place was filling up and someone was bound to notice that he had finished eating a long time ago. Dennis got up, leaving a tip on the table; he walked with measured steps to the register.

She sat on a stool with her right leg kept straight. Up close, he noticed the slight trembling of her hands and worry lines etched her face. Was it an act? He thought so. She was good, just the right amount of pathos in her voice.

The shaky smile, the right response to the inquiry of questions that were being asked.

She turned to take his ticket and he noticed her eyes. They sparkled like emeralds that had been sprinkled with gold dust. The color drained from her face, the pupils grew large, and the hand that held his ticket shook. This reaction wasn't faked, she was suddenly scared. Her eyes darted around looking for an exit or backup support. Almost in desperation, she got up and cornered another waitress, handed her the ticket and fled into the kitchen.

Rose went out the back and up the rear entrance to her apartment. She locked the door, something she seldom did. Going to the bathroom, she closed that door and sank to the floor. Those eyes and the sullen face. The scar wasn't the same but that didn't matter. The memories came back, pounding at her until she was curled up in the corner between the tub and the toilet. She could feel his hands all over her, ripping at her clothes. The stench of stale booze and cigarettes flooded her senses. She wanted to scream but couldn't for the hand of fear clamped across her mouth.

The hours slipped by and just like that night so long ago, Rose hid.

Dennis paid and left. He wasn't sure what had just happened. He caught his reflection off the car surface. With the scar, a souvenir of his last mission, he would never be called handsome or debonair. Most women he knew were curious about it, none had ever been repelled by it. What had caused the reaction? Why the fear?

Changing direction, he walked down the alley. Behind the café was a car covered over with cloth. He lifted the back of the cover; his brothers '73 Firebird with the special Tennessee license plate 'GRADY TWO' below the rear bumper. Dennis's plate was 'GRADY ONE'. That she had the car added more confusion. No one drove the 'Bird but Mark. They had spent the better part of a week and several hundred dollars rebuilding the engine. One wrong move with the foot and it could be out of control. He replaced the cover and left.

Dennis pulled into a parking lot without paying attention to which one. It was usually easy to follow a person who had a life. From what he could tell, Rose didn't have one. She lived where she worked, he couldn't follow her. Sitting in the café all day was out. Not only would it draw suspicion but also a person can only consume so much coffee.

Two women in halter tops and short shorts that showed every ripple of muscle walked by.

"Roxanne, I didn't know you were a kitchen rat. Don't get me wrong, I just never figured you for working over a hot stove all day. That was nice what you did for Pete, closing up so he could get to the hospital and see Rose. Why were you up so early on a Sunday morning?"

Roxanne smiled cattily. "I hadn't been to sleep yet."

"Oh you wicked girl!" the blonde squealed.

A slow grin spread over Dennis's face as he started the car and headed back to the motel. Dennis changed into clothes that fit the role he was going to play. Opening his brief case, he pulled out an I.D. 'Dennis Frazier, Reporter, Country Music Magazine'. The bar would be open in half an hour.

He waited an hour before stopping. There were a couple of cars in the lot. Picking up a note pad with the CMM logo on the cover he went inside. 'Leathernecks' was your typical topless bar. Pictures of the girls with flashy sequined outfits hung in the entrance. Inside it was dimly lighted. The brightest area was the runway, the stage in the middle of the room where the girls danced and performed topless to an audience of hopefully appreciative men. The runway was empty, but it wouldn't be long before more customers came in and the show would begin.

He sat down warily at the bar. Time for his own act to start. "Give me a draft please."

"Rough day?" The barmaid asked as she sat the beer in front of him.

"This humidity is killing me." He took a swallow of the cold beer and sighed. "Nothing like a cold one on a hot afternoon. Like to never found a hotel this side of town, seems like half the world is coming to Camp Lejeune."

"Where you from?" She smiled seductively. Keep 'em talking and they would stay half the night.

"Nashville, Tennessee. I'm covering the memorial ceremony for a magazine." He had her hooked now.

"We don't get many reporters in here." She filled another frosted mug and handed it to one of the girls. "Which one?"

"Country Music." He held his breath hoping he could land his prey. Things always went better if you could work with the first person you approached. Her face lit up with a big smile.

"I love country music, I wish they played it here but its not what the girls like to dance to." She glanced around for signs of empty glasses. "Why is County Music here for the ceremony?"

"Looking into doing a human interest story," Dennis felt elated. "How this effects the community, the local families and the support they get from the corps."

Dennis watched as she started laughing. "What's so funny?"

"We don't get many wives in here." She wiped the bar top with a damp towel. "But I do know of one that has a rather interesting past."

* * * * *

Gunny knocked on the door and got no response. Trying the door he found it locked. He was starting to get worried. Returning with the key he let himself in. The room was empty as was the bedroom. He opened the bathroom door and heard the whimpering. Light from the open door spilled across the floor, Rose sat curled up in the small space between the stool and the tub.

"My God Rose!" He knelt on the floor in front of her. "What's the matter? What happened?" He reached to touch her and she cowered from his touch. "Rose—Rose dear it's me, Gunny." Again she flinched when he touched her, her whimpering grew louder. Gunny didn't know what to do. Descending the stairs at a run he entered the café winded and out of breath. Cradling the phone under his chin as he dialed, he turned to Debbie.

"Rose is in her bathroom."

"Yes I need an ambulance at Gunny's café."

"I don't know what's wrong. She is hiding between the shitter and tub. She won't let me touch her."

Debbie found Rose and climbed in the tub to get closer. "Rose honey, its me Deb. Why don't you come out of there?" She smoothed Rose's damp hair away from her face. *The temperature has to be a hundred degrees in here*. She wet a washcloth and cooled Rose's flushed skin. "Everything's going to be all right Rose."

Gunny showed the ambulance crew upstairs. The EMT reached out to Rose, she flinched away from him.

"Don't," she cried, "No more, don't hurt me again."

"What's she talking about?" the driver asked.

Gunny felt helpless. "She was brutally raped at fourteen. My wife would hold for her hours after one of her nightmares. The last one that I know of was two years ago."

"She'll have be given a sedative," he explained. "She could injure herself if we tried to get her out now."

"She's pregnant also," he announced. "Her OB doctor is Cdr. Rosenthal."

"I need to use the phone," barked the EMT.

"Its downstairs in the Café." Gunny's heart was tearing him in two. "If only my wife was here."

"I'm not sure how to get her out." The ambulance driver contemplated the scene. "We may have to remove the stool. How she got herself wedged in there I can't figure out."

Gunny tore himself away long enough to get some tools and tell Pete what was going on.

* * * * *

"Hey!" A customer hollered as he walked in. "What's happened at Gunny's? There's been a ambulance there for a long time now."

Dennis felt a tightening in his gut. He didn't have to be told, he knew. The large frightened gold-specked eyes of Rose came clearly into view. He laid a ten-dollar bill on the counter and bolted through the door.

The ambulance had drawn a typical crowd of onlookers around the café. He pushed and shoved his way through the throng until he was at the door. Suddenly the door burst open and the EMT was yelling for everyone to stand back. Rose was on the stretcher, her skin flushed, an IV was being held by a Navy Lt. Commander. Dennis leaned against the window; somehow, he was responsible for this. Going inside he sat at the counter.

"I'm sorry," the waitress said. "I didn't see you come in. Things have been rather hectic around here."

"What happened? I'll just have coffee." He needed a clear head to think. For the last three hours, he had been pumping the barmaid for information and he had lost track of the beers.

"Rose had a breakdown or something." She filled his cup. "Been upstairs in her bathroom for hours. Nobody's left since Gunny found her. Everybody is waiting to find out about her."

"I take it she is well liked?"

"Liked, I would rather say loved," she corrected. "With all that girl has been through she has a heart of gold. When Gunny's wife took sick Rose stayed by her side around the clock. I'm not sure where she's from but I know after her mother died she had it bad. She lived on the street for a year before Gunny took her in. They've been like father and daughter ever since."

Dennis watched as she went to change pots and refill cups. This was beginning to fit a pattern. Growing up, Mark had brought home stray, hurt animals of one sort or another and after badgering Dennis long enough, would enlist his help in taking care of them. It was Mark who could get close to them. Only after he had soothed the little half wild creatures, could Dennis get close. Frightened, half-wild emerald eyes with powered gold dust floated through his mind.

* * * * *

Gunny felt he had aged ten years waiting for them to get Rose out. He sat in the waiting room, worried about her.

"Damn you!" he cursed aloud.

"I probably deserve that," Dennis whispered.

Gunny's head popped up. "I was referring to my wife for dying last year. Who are you?"

"I'm sorry," Dennis apologized. "I'm Dennis Grady." He saw the surprise register on Gunny's face. "Mark Grady's brother."

"Sylvester O'Toul, or just Gunny." He extended his hand and they shook.

"You don't look like your brother very much."

"Half-brother really," Dennis elaborated. "My dad was in the service, Navy. My mother didn't know what to do with me and she didn't like the long periods Dad was at sea. One day she left me at his parent's and never came back. Dad remarried and a couple years later Mark was born."

Several minutes went by as Gunny mulled over the next question. "When did you find out about the marriage?"

"Yesterday morning." Pausing for several seconds he continued. "After calling the Liaison Office."

"Came as a shock I imagine," Gunny speculated. "Why did you say you deserved the cussin' when you walked in?"

"I was in the café this morning, Rose acted fine until I handed her my ticket. She got scared. I could see it in her eyes. It was like I had grown horns and sprouted a tail."

"You had—in a way," Gunny looked at his face. "Indirectly you did cause it." He got up and walked to the window.

"How?" Dennis demanded.

"When you came out here," Gunny continued as if not hearing the question. "You didn't believe the marriage, did you? Well, yes or no?"

"All right! No! I didn't." Then in a calmer voice. "What's that got to do with this?"

"Maybe nothing—and maybe everything. I didn't know about the wedding 'til afterwards myself," he informed Dennis. "If…I hate that word, if they had gotten married sooner, and Mark could have been there when she met you, this," he moved his hand around the waiting room, "might have been avoided."

"You lost me," Dennis admitted.

"I think," Gunny uttered an oath, "I think you reminded her of, the man that—that…"

"Raped her," Dennis finished for him.

"Gunny, Rose is awake now. You can go on in." The doctor informed him. "I think she will be fine, but she needs some therapy. She has had some emotional shocks that she will need help and understanding to get over."

Gunny entered the room and watched as she stared blankly at the ceiling. He walked over to her bed and gently touched her arm. "Rose?"

She turned her head, "I saw him Gunny. He was in the café."

"Who dear?" Gunny tenderly moved an errant lock of hair from her face and placed it behind her ear.

"The man that—that raped me." She finally managed to say.

"That wasn't him Rose." Rose started to argue. "It was Mark's brother."

"Where is he?" she asked.

"Outside." Gunny waited, this had to be her decision. She had to make it on her own. Her voice had been emotionless and there was a determined intensity in her eyes as she turned to look squarely at him.

"Might as well show him in." Resolving to get through this with at least a little dignity, she sat up in bed straightening her gown and bravely signaled Gunny she was ready.

Dennis entered with hesitant steps. This was not how he pictured confronting his brother's wife. He pulled up short in the doorway. Very few people looked good lying in a hospital bed. She look better than good, she was beautiful. The gown she wore was pulled tight around her, accenting her breasts. Her eyes flickered around the room, never fully making contact with his. Rose had her hands clasped tightly together in her lap. Was it anger, fear or was she still living the nightmare that had sent her fleeing.

"So…you're Bill." He was tall, several inches above her five foot six inch height. His eyes boring into hers upset her more that she wanted to admit. "Not the most ideal place to meet ones sister-in-law."

"It's Dennis, not Bill. Bill's our father; besides, I'm the one that should be apologizing Rose. Especially, since it appears that my showing up at the café like I did caused this."

"You could have called or at least told me who you were," reasoned Rose.

"If you remember, you didn't give me a chance to say anything," he reminded. "You just ran out the door." He watched her eyes flare, was it anger or fear?

"You were in the restaurant long enough to have told someone, besides you didn't try to stop me," returned Rose.

"Would you have listened?" Dennis shot back.

"I don't think you wanted me to know." She changed her attack, going in for the kill. "Did you?"

There was no fear, only hurt, betrayal, and anger. The gold flecks sparkled, her nose flared as she breathed deeply. Her breasts lifted, straining the gown that was pulled tight around her. He forced his eyes away from the near perfection of her breasts and focused on her face.

"No, not right then." His admission hurt.

"Well, at least you're honest." Sarcastically, she added. "Now."

"Rose." Gunny admonished.

"It was Mark's idea to wait 'til he got home and we could tell you ourselves." She watched his eyes go to her waist. "Don't worry Dennis, it's Mark's. And No. I didn't trick him into marrying me. I was willing to wait, he's the one that insisted."

"Rose!" Gunny hissed.

Dennis stopped Gunny with a raised hand. "She's right, about everything. I'm sorry, I hope you'll accept my apology." Dennis turned abruptly and left.

"Kind of hard on him Rose," Gunny stated.

Rose smiled, "Not half as hard as I will be on you if you don't get me out of here."

"I'm afraid that won't be possible," Commander Rosenthal spoke from the doorway. "I want you to see another Doctor."

"Great!" she fumed. "Let me guess, a head doctor. Right?"

"She is good with rape cases, Rose." Sheala understood the reluctance, the stigma of talking to a psychologist.

"Okay, I'll go on one condition," stipulated Rose.

"What condition is that Rose?"

"That she has been raped too." She smiled at Sheala's expression. "That way when she says, Rose you poor dear, I know what a traumatic ordeal this was for you, I'll know she is telling the truth. Unless a person has been raped, they will never know what it feels like."

"Rose, she helped me." The doc's whispered words reached across the room.

They stared for what seemed like an hour, two battle hardened warriors prepared to do battle. Gunny saw the resistance break down, Rose was the first to lower her eyes. Gunny smiled.

"Okay, only it has to be in the afternoon and I'm not staying here overnight."

Dennis sat in his motel room staring at the evening news. Marine Commander Paul Kelley was in Wiesbaden Germany, handing out Purple Hearts to survivors of the bombing. He turned the set off and went for a walk.

His feet took him some hours later to the sidewalk outside Gunny's Café. Noticing the light on he went upstairs before logic and sound reasoning took over. The inside door was open. Through the screen door, he observed Rose curled up on the couch. At first, he thought she was sleeping and started to turn away. Then he heard the faint sob. Not pausing to think if he should or not he entered and crossed the room. Kneeling beside her he whispered, "Rose, it's Dennis."

"Go away," she pleaded. "Leave me alone."

There was a picture on the table. Mark and Rose on the beach. They looked so happy together, smiling faces, full of love and laughter. "Rose, I miss him too."

She turned on the couch, her cheeks were tear stained, eyes swollen and red.

"Hold me," she reached out begging for him.

Dennis was amazed at this woman. She had gone through so much and showed the world a tough side that only a die-hard marine could love. Underneath she was as her name, fragile as a rose. The warmth of her body enveloped him. He became aware of the thin cotton gown and the fact that she wore nothing underneath. He felt the fullness of her breast pressed against him. If Gunny caught him like this—that was something he couldn't let happen. Carefully lifting Rose, he carried her to her bed and left, closing the door behind him.

# Chapter Five

Dennis woke in the night. Even though the air conditioner was running full blast, he was soaked with sweat. The dream had seemed so real. Mark was standing in a ring of fire holding out an emerald. Behind him was a barrier; a curtain of light, which contained such magnificent brightness, that Dennis couldn't see what was on the other side. He took a shower and lay down, fearful for a dream that did not return.

Rose was at the counter when he walked in. "Morning Rose."

"Morning Dennis!" She lowered her voice to a whisper. "I want to thank you for being there last night."

"Don't worry Rose, your secret is safe with me," he whispered back.

A puzzled frown crossed her face. "What secret?"

"Why, that I saw what you sleep in, Rose Grady." He put his fingers to his lips. "My lips are sealed."

"I don't think so," she laughed. "I don't wear a nightgown."

"What is going on out here?" Gunny stuck his head through the swinging doors.

"Nothing Gunny," she giggled. "Just sharing family secrets."

"Humph!" He disappeared inside the kitchen.

She reached out and placed her hand on his. Their eyes locked, time stood still.

"Order up," Gunny said from the kitchen. "Rose! Order up!"

Dennis ordered; his mind wasn't on his food but her eyes, and the emerald of his dream. He shook off the nagging thought as being ludicrous, finished his coffee and paid for his meal.

"Come over for supper tonight." Gunny invited as Dennis started to leave.

* * * * *

Crossing the ally to Gunny's small but comfortable house, she ran lightly up the steps. The aroma of spicy spaghetti sauce wafted through the open door.

"Smells great, need any help?" She entered the kitchen and put her arm around his solid waist.

"You can set the table."

"Evening, Dennis." She pulled the plates off the shelf.

"I'll turn the station if it bothers you?" Dennis offered.

"I know how he died. What I don't know is why. Please leave it on."

Rose set the table and dropped wearily on the couch.

"...reporting live from Beirut. The death toll from Sunday's bombing currently stands at 260."

Dennis saw the hurt and the anguish in her face, reached over, and took her hand.

"Dozens more that were injured and have been sent to Wiesbaden, Germany for treatment and from there, to be sent home"

"Gunny…Dennis, it's been a long day." Her voice hoarse with unresolved emotions. Tears welled up making her eyes glisten. "I don't feel up to eating right now. Goodnight Dennis. See you in the morning Gunny."

Dennis visited with Gunny, gently probing him about Rose. The television was on and a Special News Alert came on.

"We take you live to the White House and the Oval Office where President Reagan is about to address the Nation."

"Some two months ago we were shocked by the brutal massacre of two hundred and sixty-nine men, women and children, more than sixty of them Americans, in the shooting down of a Korean airliner. Now, in these past several days, violence has erupted again, in Lebanon and Grenada.

"In Lebanon, we have some sixteen hundred marines, part of a multinational force that's trying to help the people of Lebanon restore order and stability to that troubled land. Our marines are assigned to the south of the city of Beirut, near the only airport operating in Lebanon. Just a mile or so to the north is the Italian contingent and not far from them, the French, and a company of British soldiers.

"This past Sunday, at twenty-two minutes after six Beirut time, with dawn just breaking, a truck, looking like many other vehicles in the city, approached the airport on a busy, main road. There was nothing in its appearance to suggest it was any different than the trucks or cars that were normally seen on and around the airport. But this one was different. At the wheel was a young man on a suicide mission.

"The truck carried some 2000 pounds of explosives, but there was no way our marine guards could know this. Their first warning that something was wrong came when the truck crashed through a series of barriers, including a chain-link fence and barbed-wire entanglements. The guards opened fire, but it was too late. The truck smashed through the doors of the headquarters building in which our marines were sleeping and instantly exploded. The four-story concrete building collapsed in a pile of rubble.

"More than two hundred of the sleeping men were killed in that one hideous, insane attack. Many others suffered injury and are hospitalized here or in Europe...."

"Nothing will come of it." There was an underlying hint of sadness and bitterness to Gunny's voice.

"Probably not, his hands are tied with all the pacifists in Congress and the Senate. Too many liberals thinking that we can deal with this on a diplomatic level."

"Probably do nothing more than lob a few bombs on the surrounding hills."

"Probably," agreed Dennis.

"... I called bereaved parents and/or widows of the victims to express on behalf of all of us our sorrow and sympathy. Sometimes there were questions. And now many of you are asking: Why should our young men be dying in Lebanon? Why is Lebanon important to us?

"Well, it's true; Lebanon is a small country, more than five-and-a-half thousand miles from our shores on the edge of what we call the Middle East. But every president who has occupied this office in recent years has recognized that peace in the Middle East is of vital concern to our nation and, indeed, to our allies in Western Europe and

Japan. We've been concerned because the Middle East is a powder keg; four times in the last thirty years, the Arabs and Israelis have gone to war. And each time, the world has teetered near the edge of catastrophe..."

Gunny got up and headed for the kitchen. "And every damn time all we do is slap a few wrists and ask them to behave."

"...For several years, Lebanon has been torn by internal strife. Once a prosperous, peaceful nation, its government had become ineffective in controlling the militias that warred on each other. Sixteen months ago, we were watching on our television screens the shelling and bombing of Beirut, which was being used as a fortress by PLO bands. Hundreds and hundreds of civilians were being killed and wounded in the daily battles.

"Syria, which makes no secret of its claim that Lebanon should be a part of a Greater Syria, was occupying a large part of Lebanon. Today, Syria has become a home for seven thousand Soviet advisers and technicians who man a massive amount of Soviet weaponry, including SS twenty-one ground-to-ground missiles capable of reaching vital areas of Israel..."

Gunny dipped a spoon full of sauce and tasted it. "The sauce is ready. Come and get it."

Dennis took his plate back to the couch. President Reagan was still speaking.

"...In the year that our marines have been there, Lebanon has made important steps toward stability and order. The physical presence of the marines lends support to both the Lebanese Government and its army. It allows the hard work of diplomacy to go forward. Indeed, without the peacekeepers from the U.S., France, Italy, and

Britain, the efforts to find a peaceful solution in Lebanon would collapse.

"As to that narrower question—what exactly is the operational mission of the marines—the answer is, to secure a piece of Beirut, to keep order in their sector, and to prevent the area from becoming a battlefield. Our marines are not just sitting in an airport. Part of their task is to guard that airport. Because of their presence, the airport has remained operational. In addition, they patrol the surrounding area. This is their part—a limited, but essential part—in the larger effort that I've described.

"If our marines must be there, I'm asked, why can't we make them safer? Who committed this latest atrocity against them and why?

"Well, we'll do everything we can to ensure that our men are as safe as possible. We ordered the battleship New Jersey to join our naval forces offshore. Without even firing them, the threat of its sixteen-inch guns silenced those who once fired down on our marines from the hills, and they're a good part of the reason we suddenly had a cease-fire. We're doing our best to make our forces less vulnerable to those who want to snipe at them or send in future suicide missions.

"We have strong circumstantial evidence that the attack on the marines was directed by terrorists who used the same method to destroy our Embassy in Beirut. Those who directed this atrocity must be dealt justice, and they will be.

"Now then, where do we go from here? What can we do now to help Lebanon gain greater stability so that our marines can come home? Well, I believe we can take three steps now that will make a difference..."

"Does he really believe that?" asked Dennis.

"Doesn't matter what he believes. All that will happen is talk, talk, and more talk with a few empty threats thrown in. "

"...First, we will accelerate the search for peace and stability in that region. Little attention has been paid to the fact that we've had special envoys there working, literally, around the clock to bring the warring factions together.

"Second, we'll work even more closely with our allies in providing support for the Government of Lebanon and for the rebuilding of a national consensus.

"Third, we will ensure that the multinational peacekeeping forces, our marines, are given the greatest possible protection...

"Typical of the government." Gunny clinched his fist in anger. "Wait for the body bags to start filling before they do anything."

"Let me ask those who say we should get out of Lebanon: If we were to leave Lebanon now, what message would that send to those who foment instability and terrorism? If America were to walk away from Lebanon, what chance would there be for a negotiated settlement, producing a unified democratic Lebanon?

"If we turned our backs on Lebanon now, what would be the future of Israel? At stake is the fate of only the second Arab country to negotiate a major agreement with Israel. That's another accomplishment of this past year, the May 17th Accord signed by Lebanon and Israel..."

"If we hadn't interfered and stopped Israel to begin with we wouldn't have a problem today." Dennis fumed.

"...Brave young men have been taken from us. Many others have been grievously wounded. Are we to tell them their sacrifice was wasted? They gave their lives in defense of our national security every bit as much as any man who ever died fighting in a war. We must not strip every ounce of meaning and purpose from their courageous sacrifice.

"We're a nation with global responsibilities. We're not somewhere else in the world protecting someone else's interests; we're there protecting our own.

"I received a message from the father of a marine in Lebanon. He told me, 'In a world where we speak of human rights, there is a sad lack of acceptance of responsibility. My son has chosen the acceptance of responsibility for the privilege of living in this country. Certainly in this country one does not inherently have rights unless the responsibility for these rights is accepted.'

"Let us meet our responsibilities."

Dennis got up and went to the kitchen for seconds.

Gunny had a smile on his face when he returned.

"What?"

"Nothing just glad that you like the chow. I used to eat like that, but had to cut back when I retired. Everything started settling around the waist."

Dennis turned his attention back to the set.

"...Sam Rayburn once said that freedom is not something a nation can work for once and win forever. He said it's like an insurance policy; its premiums must be kept up to date. In order to keep it, we have to keep working for it and sacrificing for it just as long as we live. If we do not, our children may not know the pleasure of working to keep it, for it may not be theirs to keep.

"In these last few days, I've been more sure than I've ever been that we Americans of today will keep freedom and maintain peace. I've been made to feel that by the magnificent spirit of our young men and women in uniform and by something here in our nation's capital. In this city, where political strife is so much a part of our lives, I've seen Democratic leaders in the Congress join their Republican colleagues, send a message to the world that we're all Americans before we're anything else, and when our country is threatened, we stand shoulder to shoulder in support of our men and women in the armed forces.

"May I share something with you I think you'd like to know? It's something that happened to the commandant of our Marine Corps, General Paul Kelley, while he was visiting our critically injured marines in an air force hospital. It says more than any of us could ever hope to say about the gallantry and heroism of these young men, young men who serve so willingly so that others might have a chance at peace and freedom in their own lives and in the life of their country.

"I'll let General Kelley's words describe the incident. He spoke of a young marine with more tubes going in and out of his body than I have ever seen in one body.

"He couldn't see very well. He reached up and grabbed my four stars, just to make sure I was who I said I was. He held my hand with a firm grip. He was making signals, and we realized he wanted to tell me something. We put a pad of paper in his hand... and he wrote `Semper Fi'.

"Well, if you've been a marine or if, like myself, you're an admirer of the marines, you know those words are a battle cry, a greeting, and a legend in the Marine Corps. The marine shorthand for the motto of the corps... 'Semper Fidelis'... 'Always faithful.'

"General Kelley has a reputation for being a very sophisticated general and a very tough marine. But he cried when he saw those words, and who can blame him?

"That marine and all those others like him, living and dead, have been faithful to their ideals. They've given willingly of themselves so that a nearly defenseless people in a region of great strategic importance to the free world will have a chance someday to live lives free of murder and mayhem and terrorism. I think that young marine and all of his comrades have given every one of us something to live up to.

"They were not afraid to stand up for their country or, no matter how difficult and slow the journey might be, to give to others that last, best hope of a better future. We cannot and will not dishonor them now and the sacrifices they've made by failing to remain as faithful to the cause of freedom and the pursuit of peace as they have been.

"I will not ask you to pray for the dead, because they're safe in God's loving arms and beyond need of our prayers. I would like to ask you all—wherever you may be in this blessed land—to pray for these wounded young men and to pray for the bereaved families of those who gave their lives for our freedom.

"God bless you, and God bless America."

# Chapter Six

Dennis turned the set off and sat thinking about the President's speech. "Sounds good on paper, all righteous and proper. America saving the world from oppression. Seems like I heard that same line fed to us before."

"Different time and place with a different president but same old words." Gunny stood up and took the dishes to the kitchen.

"They seem to have forgotten who was whipping who the last time the Israeli's went to war." Dennis got to his feet. "Thanks for the meal Gunny. You think Rose will be all right? Or you think I should check on her?"

"She'll be fine. Dennis, I appreciate your concern."

"Good night Gunny."

* * * * *

The next morning, Rose glanced at the clock, poured a cup of coffee, and set it on the counter by the cash register. The door opened and the mailman entered.

"Morning, Rose." He laid the mail on the counter and picked the cup up. "Rose?"

The Beirut Embassy postmark was transfixed in her mind. A mighty hand gripped her heart, ripping open the fresh wounds.

Following the line of her frozen stare to the counter top, "Gunny! You better get out here!" he yelled.

"What's all the hol…?" Rose's pale face greeted him as he left the kitchen. "Rose honey what is it?" Gunny put his arm around her and felt her shaking.

"I'm sorry Gunny," Hank apologized. "I didn't notice the postmark before."

His heart sank as he observed the letter. Reaching for the envelope Rose stopped him.

"No!" She snatched the letter and held it to her breast.

"Rose, do you want me to open it?" He gently pulled her into his arms.

This was the last thread she had. If she opened it, the last tie to a loving, living Mark would be broken. Taking a deep and shaky breath, she straightened. "Thanks Gunny but no, this is something I have to do."

"Run on upstairs dear, take all the time you need." Taking her head with both of his hands, he gently placed a kiss on her forehead.

* * * * *

Dennis woke to pounding inside his head that wouldn't go away even with his eyes open.

"Mr. Grady, phone call for you."

The pounding continued. "Okay, I'm coming! Don't beat the door down!" Dennis found the chain and opened the door.

"What?" He blinked at the bright sunlight.

"There's a call for you in the office. Your dad says it's urgent."

Putting on his pants Dennis snatched his shirt and raced to the motel office. "Dad?" He stuck the phone under his chin and fumbled with the shirt.

"Son, we just got a letter from Mark that was mailed the day before he was killed. Mother has taken it hard but I was with her. That's why I called…"

Dennis jammed his shirt into his pants as he opened the car door. Racing through the midmorning traffic, he was thankful there were no police cars around. He was out of the car before the engine had stopped running.

The front door banged open with force. Gunny was about to complain when he noticed the worried expression of Dennis's face and the disarray of his clothes. His shirt was miss-buttoned and only half tucked into his pants.

"Gunny, did Rose get a letter this morning?" He saw the small shake of Gunny's head. "My God, where is she?"

"Upstairs."

Dennis took the stairs two at a time. Without even knocking, he walked in. Rose was sitting on the couch staring at the letter in her hand. "Rose I came as quick as I could."

"Why did Gunny call you?"

"He didn't, Dad did. They got a letter this morning too. He didn't take the time to tell me what was in it. Just told me to find you before you read yours." He looked at the letter. "You haven't opened it."

"No—I'm not sure I can," her voice broke.

Dennis saw her lower lip tremble and held her hand. "When you're ready I'll be right here. I promised Dad I wouldn't leave you alone. They are both very concerned about you."

She turned her head to his shoulder as the tears came. "I'm sorry, seems like all I've done lately is cry." Within the shelter of his arms she felt safe. Strangely strengthened by his nearness Rose reached for the letter.

Dennis's arm tightened around her, pulling her closer yet to his side as she carefully broke the seal.

With trembling hands, Rose unfolded the letter. A picture fell into her lap. Turning the picture over, Mark was standing on the beach with a small fishing village nestled in the background. Every roof had dark indigo tile that glistened against a cloudless sky. Mark was smiling at the camera, water from the Mediterranean Sea lapping at his boots.

*22 October 1983*

*Dearest Rose*

*I am mailing a letter this morning to Dad and Mother. I know we were going to wait 'til I got home but have decided I can't take the risk of them not knowing. I would be lying if I told you I wasn't worried. The sniper attacks are happening on an almost daily basis. The fighting between the factions is growing worse as the date for the peace conference gets closer. Every day that we return safe from a patrol, we are thankful that we can at least sleep in relative safety.*

*Before I left there wasn't much time to talk about my family. My Dad and brother Dennis run a security business in Nashville Tennessee. I guess distrust and secrets come naturally for the whole family. Once they get to know you as I have they will love you too. I just pray that I am there beside you when that happens. Dennis handles the personal security of a number of big country stars. He will be the most difficult of the three to get close to.*

*Rose thought of where she was sitting and smiled.*

*This next is as hard for me to write, as it will be to read. If something does happen, and I don't make it home, don't shut my family out. Let them help, but don't let any of them push you into something you don't want, especially Mother. She has always run the house with a stern hand. Raising two sons with Dad running all over the world for the Naval Intelligence Service, she had too. Whatever you do, will have to be your decision. If I'm not there, I trust you to make the right decision for our child.*

*There is so much more I wanted to say but the truck going to the Embassy is about ready to leave.*

*Remember I love you.*

*Mark*

Dennis could feel the silent tremors that racked her body. Her tears splattered the pages as she silently wept for a dream that was no more. The pages blurred from his own tears as he thought of his brother fallen to a terrorist bomb. The hopes for the future swept away by a world gone mad.

*Remember I love you.* The words of the dream or was it a dream. Rose was no longer sure what was real and what was the nightmare. She picked up the picture, placing a kiss on the tip of her finger; she gently touched Mark's smiling face.

Setting the picture and the letter aside Rose awkwardly uncoiled herself from Dennis's arms. "Thank you for being here." She glanced at the time and felt dismayed. "I've got to go, it's almost lunch time." She left Dennis sitting on the couch and headed back into life.

Dennis struggled with the emotions that tore at him. His brother's death, finding out he was married. The fact that Rose was carrying Mark's child bore heavily upon him. How could he ensure that Rose was taken care of? He was building a business. Recruiting the type of people he wanted took time and money. Bodyguards couldn't be found on any street corner. Training took too long and gaining experience on the job cost lives. The people that used his services deserved the best for their money. It was his responsibility to ensure they got the best. He preyed upon disgruntled Special Forces and Navy SEALs. Occasionally he managed to lure away an agent from the Feds. Grady Security was expanding, requiring more and more time away from home setting up contracts and interviewing potential employees. He leaned his head back and closed his eyes.

The afternoon shift finally arrived and Rose was glad to be done. Trudging up the stairs after a busy and long lunch trade Rose longed for a leisurely soak in the tub. Startled at the sight of Dennis sprawled across the couch she became peeved that he had fallen asleep. *Great, now what*? Throwing her arms up in frustration, she ignored him and headed for the bath.

She had almost dozed off when she heard a voice. At first, she thought he was talking to Gunny. Something crashed to the floor. Sloshing water across the floor as she got out of the tub, she grabbed her robe and belted it around her. Dennis was trashing about on the couch. A vase of flowers was lying on the hardwood floor.

*The emerald glowed within Mark's hand, as crimson tongues of fire leapt around him. They held him captive and would not let him go. Again, Mark held out the emerald.*

*"No Mark, I can't. I can't."*

"Dennis, wake up." She grabbed his shoulder and gently shook him.

*"Damn you Mark." Mark was gone, stepping into the blinding light. Dennis looked and all around him, the fire clung. In his hand was the emerald.*

"Dennis! Wake up!" She shook him until his head bounced off the arm of the couch. His eyes flew open. She was taken back by the wildness in them. Her arms were hurting where he held them in an iron grip. "You were having a dream. Please let go, you're hurting my arms."

"More like a nightmare," he moaned. Dennis looked at where he held Rose's arms. "I'm sorry, I didn't mean to hurt you." His eyes were hypnotized by the perfect roundness of her breast.

Rose saw the hunger in his eyes. She pulled the robe together, now if she could just gather her thoughts in the same way. "I was taking a ah—I heard a noise—I swear this isn't—this isn't what you think."

The dampness of her skin had made the thin material nearly transparent. The darkened nipples were visible. "You don't know what I'm thinking." He got up and quickly turned from Rose. "I'll talk to you later. Good night."

The words of her father came back to her. "*You're just like your Mother! A cheap little tramp that will do anything to trap a man.*" Shame and humiliation swept over her. Picking up the picture, she cradled it her breast. Curling into a little ball on the couch that was still warm from Dennis's body, she fell into an exhausted sleep.

* * * * *

The doubts returned as Dennis walked along Court Street. What he knew and thought warred within him. Not disputing Mark had loved Rose, or at least had been in love with the idea of love. He wondered how the two had gotten together. Had she tempted him with sweet promises of passionate nights? Her perfection was etched upon his mind as permanently as a Greek goddess carved in stone. Rational reasoning shattered at the certainty he felt, the emerald in his nightmare was his brother's wife. Dawn was quickly approaching as he opened his motel door. Sleep deprived and emotionally exhausted he laid down on the bed.

* * * * *

Rose took off her apron and melted into a booth seat. The morning rush hour had continued into the noon mealtime. Debbie plopped down in the other seat with a heavy sigh. "Feels good just to be able to sit for a change," Rose stated.

"Feels damn good. You realize that this is the first time either of us has been off our feet all morning. Rose, your leg must be giving you hell right now. Thought the Doc told you to take it easy for a few days? The marathon we ran today doesn't qualify."

Rose laughed wearily and watched as Gunny carried a pot of coffee and three cups over to the booth. He looked tired, his face flushed from the heat of the kitchen and the continuous stream of meals he had prepared. He looked every bit his fifty-nine years with an extra couple of decades added on.

"Girls, I have come to a conclusion. I am going to advertise for some help in the kitchen and for another waitress. I'm not getting any younger and you," he pointed to Rose, "are not following the Doc's orders."

"Excuse me."

Rose looked up at the woman speaking. "Hi, Commander. What brings you out this way?"

"I was wondering if I might have a few words with you?"

Debbie stood up. "I need to be going anyway. See you tomorrow Rose, you too Gunny."

"Please stay." Rose placed her hand on Gunny's arm as he started to get up.

"Please have a seat," invited Rose.

"One of the duties I have on the base, other than being a Doctor, is working with the Casualty Assistance Office. When I knew Mark's name was on the list of casualties I asked to be assigned to you.

"Rose, first off I want to say again, on behalf of the commanding officer of Camp Lejeune and the city of Jacksonville how terribly sorry we are for your loss. There are, unfortunately, some forms that need your signature. Also, I have some information that will be helpful for you. My job is to assist you in any way I can.

"Rose, I know you are hurting. You keep working; you put on a smile much as you do your apron. You aren't alone in this. There's a group of women in the community that have gone through what you and so many others are facing. Several of them have gotten together and formed a group called the 'Beirut Connection.' They are working with the Casualty Assistance Office to help all the families connected with last Sunday's attack."

Gunny held up his cup, signaled Debbie, and pointed to Sheala.

When the cup was placed on the table, she smiled her thanks, taking a sip. She opened a manila envelope, pulling out several papers before continuing.

"This is the Report of Casualty form. It shows proof of death to government and commercial agencies that pay benefits to survivors. It contains all the information of Mark's service."

"I have a check for you Rose." She handed Rose the check and watched as her eyes opened wide.

"Is this the insurance money?"

"No, that is a Death Gratuity payment. It's to help in your immediate financial assistance. All I need is your signature stating you have received it."

Rose signed the receipt and handed it back to Sheala.

"This form is to receive Mark's money that he had due him. I'll help you fill it out and then forward it to the finance office. It should take two to three months to process before you get the check from them. Your claim forms for his insurance should be here in about a week. I'll help you fill them out and get them sent in for you."

Rose looked at each form that Sheala brought out. She was glad that there was someone who knew and understood what they were all for. One especially caught her attention.

"Let me get this straight. Even if I remarry, Mark's child will still be able to receive benefits 'til the age of eighteen?"

"Yes, as long as Mark is named as the father on the birth certificate. You can shop for him at the Navy Exchange; the child can use all the base facilities. Mark's child will have all the privileges of a regular dependent. Your base privileges will, however, stop should you remarry unless your new husband has those privileges himself."

Rose looked at Sheala and saw compassion in her eyes. She somehow knew the next question would be about Mark.

"Have you thought about funeral arrangements Rose?"

"I…I can't make those. Contact his parents in Nashville. Mark was only mine for a short time." She blinked back the tears that filled her eyes. Taking a napkin she wiped at the ones that escaped and flowed down her cheeks.

"You're sure about this? This is what you want?"

"Yes."

"Alright, I'll contact the Veterans Affairs Office in Nashville. They will contact his parents and convey your desire that they handle the arrangements."

"Thank you," Rose replied.

"I think that about covers everything for now. When the other papers come in, I'll get back in touch. Rose if you need anything," she stood up to leave. "Call me, okay."

Rose sat there looking over the papers stacked up in front of her. Tears trickled down her cheeks as the overwhelming realization of their meaning hit her with a fresh wave of sorrow and grief.

Gunny slid next to her and put a comforting arm around her. "My precious Rose, I know it's hard to loose someone like this. It's close to shift change. Debbie can handle anything that comes up. Go on upstairs and rest."

"Thanks." She placed a kiss on his cheek. "Gunny…I love you."

"I love you too Rose."

As he turned toward the kitchen she saw a big tear drop escape from the corner of his eye. Rose sat in her room looking out the window at life as it went on around her. *I wonder what Dennis is doing.* She hadn't seen him all day.

* * * * *

Rose turned the television on the next morning.

"We go live to Beirut for an update on the crisis in the Middle East."

"The death toll from last Sunday morning's attack has climbed to 265. A spokesman for the marines told me there are still six marines unaccounted for. They do not expect them to be found alive. Some of the marines have already begun their final trip home. For that report we go live to Dover Air Force Base at Dover, Delaware."

"At Dover Air Force Base, there is a somber gray cloud of grief and bitterness. Arriving this morning is the first of many aircraft bringing home marines killed in the terrorist bombing last Sunday morning. They are being met by the Marine Honor Guard and senior marine headquarters personnel. In a short ceremony, General Paul Kelley praised the fallen troops for their dedication, bravery and sacrifice for the cause of freedom.

"What we are wondering through all this, where are the president and vice president? Even the president's cabinet members have failed to make an appearance today.

"For an update on the wounded marines we turn now to our reporter at Camp Lejeune."

"In Camp Lejeune on this Saturday morning the first group of marines wounded in last Sunday's bombing will be arriving in just under an hour. Parents and loved ones are waiting anxiously for their return. On board is one marine that was mistakenly reported as killed. His parents are grateful to have him alive."

Rose tuned out the rest of the news broadcast. She forced her mind to other thoughts, the order she carried to a table, the customer who just entering the café. Where was Dennis? He was avoiding her and she couldn't blame him. Maybe it was best this way. She was on her own, just like always. Well, not really alone, she still had Gunny. Rose felt warmth from within. *Yes my sweet child, I still have you.*

Exhaustion dogged her steps at the end of the day. Her body was changing but she didn't have time to adjust to those changes. Rose unbuttoned her blouse and sighed with relief as the clasp of her bra loosened. Monday she had to get bigger bras. She had to talk to Gunny about getting some air conditioning up here. Even with a fan going the heat was intense. She undressed and stepped into the shower. The cool water was wonderfully refreshing.

Dennis knocked and waited. He must have driven past the café a hundred times. Thanks to the nightmare he had, and a feeling of responsibility for his brother's wife, he had been plagued with a couple of sleepless nights and indecisive days. Even now, standing outside Rose's door, he wanted to run. She might not even be home. The street door was locked. He hadn't bothered checking to see if the car was out back. Entering through the private entrance in the café, he climbed the stairs. Dennis pushed against the screen door and it opened.

Rose walked into the living room with head down while wrapping her wet hair in a towel. Flipping the end of the towel over her shoulder she came face to face with Dennis.

"Get out!" Rose screamed. "How dare you just walk into my house? Who do you think you are that you can just walk in here any time you want?"

"I knocked, the door was unlocked." The sight of her nearly astounded him. Droplets of water were still clinging like dew to the petals of a flower. The crimson curls below her waist glistened like diamonds in the sun.

"Well, you didn't knock loud enough and the doors are locked. If you are referring to the door from the café, you had better learn to read. It says 'PRIVATE Do Not Enter' and that is exactly what it means."

"Rose." Dennis tried to calm her. "Go put some clothes on, we need to talk."

"This is my place!" she yelled. Rose stared Dennis in the eye, her hands resting on her hips. She'd be damned if any one was going to intimidate her in her own apartment. "If I want to walk around naked all day that's my privilege. We are through talking, Dennis, get the hell out. Now!"

# Chapter Seven

"Rose!" Pete's voice came from the stairs. "Are you all right?"

"Yes, Pete, I'm fine."

"Just thought that you might want to know that as loud as you're yelling, everyone on the strip knows Dennis is up there and you're not wearing any clothes."

The laughter in Pete's voice infuriated Rose that much more. "Shut up Pete and go back to the kitchen."

"Dennis, leave!"

"On one condition," he bargained.

"Anything as long as you leave," she uttered before thinking.

"Great," he beamed. "I'll be back in an hour, be ready."

"For what?" she demanded.

"I'm taking you out to dinner." As Rose started to speak he stopped her. "You said anything, I'm leaving. One hour."

* * * * *

Rose stood staring at her meager wardrobe knowing that she really had only one dress.

When the doorbell sounded, Rose had no choice but to let him in. Wearing only her bra and panties she sat down to wait. What difference did it make that she wasn't dressed? Dennis had seen it all anyway.

Dennis stepped in the door and stopped, not believing what he saw. "You're not dressed?"

"My, you're observant. Is it that obvious?" she sniped sarcastically. "I'm not going." He had on gray slacks and a short sleeve pastel blue shirt that was stretched tight across his chest. With Dennis looking like he stepped out of an advertisement for men's casual wear, there was no way. "I don't have anything to wear."

"That's ridiculous," he laughed. "Every woman says that and her closet is full." He started for the bedroom.

"Where do you think you are going?" Rose stood and stepped in front of him. "You just can't walk in here and go pawing through my things. I said I didn't have anything to wear out to dinner."

He walked around her and into the bedroom.

"Dennis," she pleaded. "Please, don't do this."

He gawked in amazement at the closet. Uniform skirts and blouses for the café, a couple blouses for casual wear but nothing that gave any hint of a social life. In the back corner, almost hidden was a shimmer of white. Dennis pulled the other clothes back to reveal a white dress of medium length, puffy short sleeves with frilly lace, and a modest bust line.

Dennis carried the dress back into the living room. "You were almost right, I found this." He held out the dress. "I've never seen a woman's closet with so little in it before."

"Damn you, Dennis," she slumped to the couch. "Why couldn't you have just left or something? Why did you have to go snooping into things that don't concern you?"

Dennis was taken aback by her attitude. What had he done now?

"You, with all your money and fancy clothes, might not understand this so I'll make it plain and simple." She refused to cry. "The reason that is the only dress in the closet is because I bought it for my wedding." Rose turned her back to him and walked over to the window.

Dennis looked at the dress that was draped over his arm and then at the slender back of Rose. *What a heel he was.* He carried the dress back to the closet and hung it up. Rose was still standing in front of the window. Walking over to her, he placed his hands on her shoulders.

"Rose," his voice barely above a whisper, "I'm sorry."

How easy it would be to turn and find comfort in his arms. She pushed the thought aside. "Don't be, I don't want your pity." The warmth of his hands was weakening her resolve.

"I think you ought to go, Dennis." She closed her eyes. Tears welled up and slowly trickled down each cheek.

"Here," he handed her a blouse and a worn pair of jeans. "Put these on and we'll go."

Rose turned around and grabbed the clothes. "If you don't care, why should I?" She pulled her jeans up and zipped them shut, thankful that he had at least picked a pair that had been too large. *When was that, a month or two months ago?* She thought to herself.

"Those straps are starting to cut into your shoulders," he observed.

"I hadn't noticed." She slipped the blouse on and buttoned it. "You ready?"

They got in Dennis's car; he paused with his hand on the key. "Rose, why are there only work clothes in your closet?"

"I never needed anything else." She buckled her seat belt. "Are we going?"

"It looks like you need a few things now. The memorial ceremony is in a few days, plus the funeral will be in Nashville after that."

"For your information, I'm going shopping Monday. I know what is required. I won't embarrass you or your family by my shabby clothes."

"Rose, what about your embarrassment?"

"That's a laugh, Dennis. When you have to wear an old ragged flea-infested coat to stay warm, scavenge through people's garbage cans, and stand in soup lines, you might be able to relate. 'Course if you slept in an old cardboard box in some back alley, you wouldn't be afraid of being raped only to find the next morning that some wino pissed on you while you were sleeping. Don't you worry about me being embarrassed."

Groaning, Dennis rested his head on the back of the seat. "I'm sorry Rose."

"Why should you be sorry? It wasn't your fault," she scoffed. "I went on the streets of my own free will. Yeah, I was raped and I will never forget it or know who did it. If I had stayed at home, it would have happened anyway and I would have always known. Life on the street was not easy but it was better than what I had. If we are going to eat you need to start the car."

Dennis started the car. "I am new in town, where would you like to go."

"If you like seafood the Fisherman's Wharf is an excellent place," she suggested.

Dennis heard the lift to her voice and saw her bright smile. Sunlight caught her hair causing it to glow as if it were on fire. It took so little to make her smile. If just for an hour, he could help her forget the pain and loss. He just couldn't forget Rose was his brother's wife, carrying his brother's child.

"The Wharf it is. Which way?"

"Take a left to Murrill, then North to US 17, and make a left. The Wharf is on Marine Boulevard South. It's on the water."

Dennis pulled into the parking lot ten minutes later. The restaurant was a low building built on the edge of New River. It was a long building painted in blue with round porthole-type windows along the parking lot side. A wooden pier reaching out into the river was lighted.

"I love the salt air and the wide open ocean." She inhaled the ocean breeze that swept up the river. "Growing up, the ocean was my refuge. I would sit for hours on Atlantic Beach with my feet buried in the sand, watching the big ships sail by, headed out to sea. The Mayport Jetties was another favorite of mine. I would dream I was on one of those Navy ships headed off to wonderful exotic places overseas."

Inside, the Wharf was decorated in a nautical motif. A small store on the left offered shells, T-shirts, and souvenirs of North Carolina and the "Famous Fisherman's Wharf". Fishing nets, hung on ropes, ran along the top of the windows that faced the water. Ship's wheels converted into lights were suspended from the ceiling. Booths and small tables filled the dining areas.

Watching sadness dim her smile Dennis felt a chill. The sensation was a reveling one. "Mark brought you here didn't he?"

She startled, "How did you know?"

"Lucky guess. Shall we sit outside and eat." Dennis motioned to a row of booths that lined the edge of the boardwalk outside the building. Going outside he stopped at a table.

Rose sat and looked around. "Why this table when there are others available? You singled out this table like a shark. How do you explain the coincidence of not only bringing me to the same restaurant but also sitting at the same table Mark did the night he asked me to marry him?"

The waitress came stopping further comment. After ordering their drinks, Rose got up and went to the buffet table.

Dennis was left with nothing to do but follow. He watched as Rose filled her platter with steamed oysters and crabs, then add a large handful of chilled shrimp to an already heaping pile of food.

Picking up a crab she cracked it open and dug out the succulent white meat. "I'm waiting for an answer."

He peeled a shrimp and stared at it and then at Rose, "I don't know." Dennis popped the shrimp in his mouth. "You chose the place to eat."

"You chose the seat," she countered.

"I liked the view." Dennis felt himself responding physically when she unconsciously sucked the sauce off a peeled shrimp.

"Is something wrong?" She whispered across the table.

"No, why?" He went back to his food.

"You were staring." Taking an oyster, she savored the flavor of the meat.

"Sorry." He tried to avoid eye contact with her the rest of the meal but found it increasingly difficult to do.

Rose was on her second platter of food when she noticed Dennis again watching her. "Why are you looking at me like that?"

"I was just watching the lights reflect off your hair," he smiled. "You have beautiful hair."

"Thank you, my mother's hair was the same."

"You ought to do that more often," he teased.

"Do what more often?"

"Smile like that," he softly answered. "When you do, your whole face lights up and your eyes sparkle like jewels."

"Now I know you're Mark's brother." She almost choked with laughter. She took a sip of water. "He used to spout off the same nonsense."

Rose pushed the almost empty platter away with a satisfied sigh. "I can't eat another bite." She wiped her hands on the linen towel.

Dennis paid the bill and they walked out on the pier. The sun was just dropping over the distant mountains blazing the sky with red, blue, and golden bands of light. "You want to go for a walk and then maybe take in a movie?"

"A walk sounds good," she sighed. "Can we go to the beach?"

"Sure, let's go."

Dennis drove the few miles to the beach and parked. Rose got out and taking a deep breath, brushed her hair back and up with her hands as she stretched.

He watched anxiously as her breasts pulled tight against her blouse. Knowing what she looked like, this picture of her with the rolling white caps and sea gulls gave him a desire he knew was wrong.

Slipping off her shoes she held out her hand, "You ready?"

Against his own sound reasoning and logic he took her hand, not letting go as they walked along the foamy edge of the breaking waves.

"I don't know where the time has gone." Dennis observed the stars and the receding tide. "Maybe we should take in a movie another time."

"That might be best," she agreed. "I'm off Monday so tomorrow night would be good."

Returning to the car, he opened the door for her, his arm brushed across her breast. By the light from inside the car, he saw the flair within her eyes and heard the sharp intake of breath. The ride back to Gunny's was quiet as he reflected upon the evening. He didn't want to have feelings for Rose other than those of a brother-in-law. What was he going to do now that he did? If you're smart you'll stay away, his mind told his heart. This was for the best, but his heart wasn't listening.

*There is no future in this. After the funeral Dennis will be in Nashville and I will still be here with Gunny.* Saying the words in her mind didn't help. Believing them to be true didn't change the attraction she felt. The spiel about being family would change in time to mean Mark's poor widow. She didn't want his or their pity. With the money from

Mark's insurance, and what she had saved, their child would be assured of an education and not have to beg on the streets. Mark's baby growing inside her was the one imperative consideration that she must always keep in focus.

Arriving at Gunny's Dennis opened her door and walked Rose to the door. "Good night, Rose," he whispered. He brushed his knuckles lightly down the side of her face. Knowing it was right to walk away didn't make it easy. It wasn't what he wanted to do.

## Chapter Eight

The next morning, when Rose turned the television on, the news had already started.

"Even as peace talks in Geneva, Switzerland prepare to open tomorrow between the warring factions of Lebanon, the attacks in Beirut continue to place marines in harm's way. Two more marines were wounded yesterday in the continued fighting.

"Representatives Montgomery, Richardson, Dyson, and Hammerschmidt have come out publicly and criticized the Marine Corps for the lack of security at the marine barracks in Beirut. Retired Admiral Robert Long is expected to be heading the investigation concerning the security and the marines continued roll in Lebanon.

"Closer to home, more bodies of fallen marines from Beirut and Grenada continue to arrive at Dover Air Force Base. Not since Vietnam have we seen this many flag-draped caskets lined up on the floor of this huge hanger."

Disturbed by the news, Rose forced her mind away from Mark's body lying on the floor of a hanger in Dover. The only other topic her mind could focus on was her outing with Dennis last night and the prospect of seeing him tonight. There was an attraction, a current, which alarmed and at the same time intrigued her.

* * * * *

Hurrying through her shower, Rose finished dressing as Dennis knocked on the door. "Almost ready." She brushed her hair one last stroke. "You let me pick last night, so tonight it's your turn to choose."

"How about Flashdance?" He suggested as he held the door. "It's a new release and supposed to be good?"

"Sounds great, it's playing not far from here." She gave the directions and soon had Dennis pulling into the parking lot.

Somewhere during the movie, Rose realized they were holding hands. It was an unconscious happening that if Dennis was aware of he wasn't showing any outward sign. Other than shifting around in his seat as if he were uncomfortable, he appeared engrossed in the movie.

After the movie, on the way back to her apartment, a part of him didn't want this night to end. His sane rational mind shouted that it must. Arriving outside Gunny's he got out and opened her door. Taking her hand seemed the natural thing to do. Rose unlocked the door, looked up, and smiled. He gravitated without thought to her mouth and kissed her. The kiss was light at first.

Just an innocent goodnight kiss that ended up leaving them short of breath.

"This is a mistake that neither one of us can afford to make Dennis. Thank you for the movie. Goodnight." Closing the door, she leaned against the wall, her legs no longer solid beneath her.

Leaning against the door that Rose had just locked behind her, Dennis took some deep breaths to calm his racing heart that was pumping liquid fire through his veins. He wasn't sure if there was a word vile enough to describe what he had just done. Mark wasn't even in the grave and he was on the verge of taking her to bed. *Where had these thoughts come from? What sinister evil had invaded his mind and taken over his body?* Even now just the thought of her stirred the coals of desire, sending little specks of fire dancing upon the winds of his mind. Muttering an oath that wasn't adequate, he got in the car and drove off.

Hearing the car drive away Rose climbed the stairs. They seemed longer tonight for some reason. Why, she asked herself did she have to return the kiss. Return, she had returned it all right. Participated and encouraged it in reckless abandon right on the sidewalk. It was a good thing that the kiss had happened outside. If they had been in her apartment, she knew exactly where they would have ended up. She felt a fleeting sense of disappointment.

*You're just like your mother.*

"I'm not. I'm not." Sprawled across the bed and she covered her head, trying to shut out her father's hateful words.

Bloodshot eyes stared back at her from the mirror. The morning sun was already well into the sky signaling that she was late. Monday the café was closed to customers but that didn't mean her work was done. Inventory needed to be ordered and the books gone over but this morning she wished it wasn't hers to do. Looking longingly at the tub, she turned the shower on and stripped out of her clothes. She hated sleeping in her clothes, after sleeping in them for a year; she liked the freedom of sleeping nude. Stepping into the shower, she let the hot spray soak away the stiffness.

Gunny was in the storage room when she went down. "Morning Gunny." She picked up the clipboard. "Sorry, I overslept."

"I was going over the inventory. You want some breakfast?" Gunny turned and eyed Rose. She was wearing a pair of rumpled jeans and t-shirt that looked like they had been slept in; it was what she wasn't wearing that raised an eyebrow. "You get dressed in a hurry this morning girl? You seem to have forgotten something."

"I've got to get new ones today, mine are cutting into my shoulders," she commented. "Even my pants are getting too tight. I gave up trying to find another pair that fit and put these back on."

"You'll also need some clothes for the Memorial Service on Friday." Gunny put his arm around her shoulder. "You need to eat. Afterward I'll take the inventory and you can do the books and go. It's been a while since you went shopping. Maggie would skin me alive if she saw your closet. Lord knows I've tried to give you more for things like that but all you do is push it away." Reaching into his pocket, he pulled out his billfold.

"No Gunny…"

"Hush," he interrupted her. "I'm going to give you this and you are going to spend every dime on clothes. I'll not have a daughter of mine going without some decent dresses. Don't argue with me. Maggie would want this."

"Thanks Gunny." She tuned away to hide the moisture that was building and wiped her eyes.

Halfway though their meal they heard someone pounding on the door. Ignoring the person, they continued to eat. The knocking continued with increased volume.

"Damn." Gunny got up mumbling. "Can't they read the sign?"

Reaching the door, he found not one person but a large number of people with cameras, microphones, and several news vans outside. Gunny swore more fluently and returned to the counter. Taking an apron, he tossed it to Rose. "There's a group of reporters outside and I don't think they're going to leave. Please put this on."

Rose slipped on the apron as Gunny went back to the door.

Half an hour later, the last reporter expressed their sympathy and left. Rose felt drained; the questions had been personal and painful to answer. Somehow, she had managed without breaking down.

"My Maggie always said 'When things get you down, go shopping.' Running this business with me she went shopping a lot," he started laughing. "She never bought much but she was always in a better mood when she came back. Go ahead and do your shopping girl. When you get back we'll hit those books."

Rose started to leave.

"Rose," he stopped her. "I'm real proud of you. The way you handled the interview. Maggie would be too."

"Thanks Gunny." Smiling she headed to the back parking lot and Mark's car. She knew what he meant. Three years ago, she would have turned the air blue with her street language. Thanks to Maggie most of that was gone.

Pulling into the parking lot of the Jacksonville Mall, she received a catcall upon stepping from the car. Almost flipping the bird at the man she smiled instead. Catching her reflection in a window, she decided which store to visit. Going past several stores she made Claire's Boutique her first stop. While standing in front of a rack of clothing, a woman with a bright smile approached.

"Good Morning," she inquired. "May I help you?"

"Please, this is the first time for me," seeing the confusion on the woman's face she added. "At being pregnant." Rose noticed a man in the store but didn't pay much attention to him. "My other bras are just getting too tight."

"These would be the best." The woman stepped over to another section. "They have the wider support at the shoulders and underneath for when you really start putting on the weight."

Rose caught a glimpse of the man again. He was starring openly at her and actually leaning toward them. Turning, she snapped. "What's the matter mister? Your hearing aid broke or do you need new glasses?" The man quickly turned away and left the store.

Finishing her purchase she headed down the mall corridor.

Passing Western's Wear Head Quarters she entered Belks.

An hour later, a new and improved version of Rose walked out of the store. She had to admit the new outfit created a buoyancy she hadn't felt since Mark's death. She had used Gunny's two hundred dollars, added another one to it and she still needed shoes.

Rose stood in front of the window display of Shoe Show. The image staring back still surprised her; Indigo knee length skirt and a white sleeveless blouse with a lace overlay and moderate V-neck that ended just above the lacy bra that she had purchased earlier. Resolved that there was no other way around it she entered the store.

"May I help you, Miss?" The clerk's tone was of the utmost respect.

"Yes, I am interested in something for casual evening wear that can also be used for a more formal setting."

She finally settled on a pair of black pumps and loafers.

Setting in the dining area of the Mall eating a light lunch, Dennis was drawn to a beautiful woman with her arms loaded down with packages. To think that there could be two women in the same town with hair the same remarkable color. One plain with no polish or elegance and this one looking like she had just stepped out of a women's fashion magazine. By the number of packages she carried, it was obvious she liked to stay in style.

She turned around and he couldn't believe what or who he was looking at. Rose? No, it couldn't be. She waved at him and smiled. It was. Dennis wasn't sure what was going on but he definitely liked the results.

"Hi Dennis! You mind if I set this stuff here while I get something to drink?" She watched him nod to a chair where she promptly dumped her packages. "Be right back."

Rose paid for her cappuccino and came back to the table. Seeing his appreciative smile, she turned in a slow circle. "Well, what do you think?"

"I think," he chuckled. "That you went shopping, and that you look very lovely."

"I feel lovely!" Pulling out a chair and she sat the cup on the table. "I just wish that I was buying them for a different reason."

"I know." Dennis pushed the empty tray aside. "I talked to Dad this morning. The funeral will be next

Monday. They will fly back right after the Memorial Service here and they're hoping you can go back with us."

"That's fine. I told the base to have your parents make all the arrangements." Rose sipped her cappuccino in an effort to wash away the sudden lump in her throat.

"Mother is handling this better with something to do and it gives her a sense of purpose in this difficult time." Dennis saw the sadness creep back into her eyes. "So, other than shopping, how has your morning been?"

"We had several reporters this morning at the café. Somehow they found out that I had recently gotten married to Mark and wanted to interview me." She finished her drink and stood. "Figured it was better to have a interview in the empty café rather than have them come back tomorrow."

"Here." He stood with her. "Let me help you with those."

Dennis felt his heart shudder when she flashed him a radiant smile.

* * * * *

Three hundred miles to the south in the city rescue mission the TV was playing. An unshaved man with dirty clothes was waiting for his only meal of the day. His hands were fumbling with his lighter. He was out of cigarettes and he needed a drink.

"Mrs. Grady, we understand that you and Sergeant Mark Grady had only recently gotten married," the reporter stated.

"We were married on September 8, the day he shipped out," replied Rose. "We weren't even able to have any pictures because he had to leave."

All thought of food, cigarettes or even alcohol fled from his mind as he viewed the answer to all his problems.

"How long have you worked at Gunny's Café?" asked another reporter. "What are your plans now?

I've been here three years and I have no plans other than bury my husband, work here, and raise our child," she smiled into the camera.

"Yes I am expecting. Mark was to be home just before my delivery date," she wiped a tear away.

"We understand that you received a letter mailed the afternoon of the twenty-second. Would you share that letter with the nation?"

"I'm sorry, I can't read it right now," her lips quivered. "It's still to painful. Gunny can read it if he will. It's up to him."

He stood watching the set as the letter was read. As soon as he finished eating, he was headed north.

* * * * *

Thursday morning Rose woke to a gray and forbidding sky. A fine drizzle coated everything in a blanket of mist. Taking extra care with her attire, she went downstairs to meet Mark's parents.

"Mother, Dad," Dennis made the introductions. "I would like you to meet Rose, Mark's wife.

"Please dear enough with formalities." She took Rose's hand. "It's Shalinn and I'm so sorry we couldn't have met for a happier occasion."

"I'm Bill." Her father-in-law took her hand. "Why don't we all sit down? It might be a little less awkward."

Rose led them to a back table that had been reserved.

Shalinn was a beautiful, warm, but commanding woman. Even though she was only slightly taller than Rose, she seemed to tower over her. Her white hair glistened in the morning light, adding to the sparkle from the diamond earrings that hung suspended from each lobe. Bill on the other hand, when she looked up at him, was taller than Dennis. With his stern, tight-lipped smile and eyes that were unwavering in his appraisal of her, she felt guilty of something just being in his presence.

Debbie came with a coffee decanter and set it on the table. "Rose, when you're ready to order just let me know."

"Rose, I know this has been a difficult time for you." Shalinn clasped Rose's hand. "It has been for all of us. I want to thank you for allowing me to take care of all the arrangements. Without that to take care of, I might have fallen apart."

"Shalinn and I are pleased that you have decided to come back with us for a few days. It will give us a chance to get to know each other." Bill patted her hand in a comforting gesture.

"Rose." Shalinn had tears in her eyes. "How did you and Mark meet?"

"He came in, one Sunday morning, and had breakfast. We visited for a few minutes. He started coming by after I got off work and we would sit here and talk. He finally persuaded me to go for a walk down the street for an ice cream. Then on the Fourth of July we went to watch the fireworks display down at the marina," pausing she poured coffee for each.

"And that's the night you got pregnant?" Shalinn asked.

"I—I don't know." Rose refused to show any embarrassment.

"Rose, dear," Shalinn patted her arm, "from Mark's letter I know he loved you. That's all that matters."

The front door opened and a beggar came in, Rose looked up and saw his face.

Debbie watched the beggar as he walked across the room. Something about his grin sent a disturbing chill up her spine. Stepping into the kitchen, she warned Gunny. "I think you better get out here. Look like trouble with a homeless, he's not one of the regulars from around here."

Dennis was instantly aware that something was wrong. The color went from her face and her eyes had that same look of fear. "Rose, what's wrong?"

Bill and Shalinn exchanged bewildered looks.

The beggar stopped short of the table and smiled, "Hello Rose, it's been such a long time. Don't you want to introduce me to your friends? I'm Richard Shawnassy, Rose's dad." He reached out to shake hands.

Stepping through the batwing doors, Gunny saw the frightened look on Rose's face.

Dennis stood, ignoring Richard's outstretched hand. "I think its time for you to leave, Rose doesn't want to see you and neither do I."

"Well that's tough because I came all this way to see my daughter and I intend to," he boasted.

"Looks like you've done just that." Gunny spoke from behind him. "Leave like you were told or I'll throw you out."

"You can't throw me out." Richard puffed out his chest with false bravado. "I know my rights. I came in here to have a cup of coffee and see my daughter." Pulling out a chair, he started to sit when the chair was pushed out from under him. Looking up from the floor where he sprawled he saw Rose glaring down at him.

"Out." She gestured to the door. "Don't come back, don't write, and don't call. You haven't been my father for over four years."

Richard climbed unsteadily to his feet. "Rose darling let me make those years up to you."

Smack! The sound of the slap across his face left everyone stunned. "I am not your darling!" The fear had turned to anger that was becoming a force of rage inside her.

"Gunny!" She spoke without taking her eyes off Richard. "Throw this sorry good-for-nothing bum's ass out of here and if he shows up again call the police."

"Why you ungrateful little bitch." Richard snarled, raising his fist. "You're just like your mother, nothing but a tramp and a cheap whore…"

A solid fist connected with the side of Richard's jaw cutting off any further insults.

Dennis stood over the prone figure of Rose's dad, his fist still clenched.

"Thanks," Gunny mumbled. "Saved me the trouble. Give me a hand, if he hasn't come to by the time the police get here they can have him."

Together Dennis and Gunny dragged Richard outside.

Dennis came back to find Rose being consoled by his mother. He could see the controlled anger that radiated from his dad. "Shall we order? I don't know about anyone else but I'm starved."

The encounter with Richard dampened the conversation around the table. They ate in relative silence, each lost in their own thoughts concerning the unwelcome intrusion.

"Mother and Dad want to go out to the base and look around. Would you like to go with us?" Dennis broke the silence.

"That would be nice," she smiled at Shalinn. "I hope you're not expecting a grand tour of the base. I've only been there a couple of times and that was to the hospital and to the beach with Mark."

"We just want to spend some time with you my dear so we can get to know one another." She patted Rose on the hand and returned the smile.

Shalinn and Rose sat in the back while Dennis drove. Pulling out of the parking lot, his dad tapped his arm and with a shift of the eyes and a slight jerk of the head directed his attention across the street. Just moving into the deeper shadows of an alley was a scurrying figure.

At the main entrance of the base, Dennis stopped to obtain a pass and a map. Driving down Holcomb Blvd he turned onto Virginia Dare Dr. past two story brick buildings.

"This area was the women's training area during World War II." Rose read the base tour guide. "Of the twenty thousand or so women that joined the corps most were trained right here."

They went past the St. Frances Xavier Catholic Chapel, there was a large gathering with a hearse backed up to the door. Turning on McHugh Boulevard, they went out towards the old hospital. Heading back towards the center of the base, they went past the Second Marine

Division. Preparations were under way for Friday's ceremony. Back on Holcomb, they went past Building One, the Headquarters for the Commanding General of Camp Lejeune. The building was swarming with high-ranking Marine Officers and Staff personnel.

"With President Reagan here Friday this place will be a mad house all night long." Bill spoke with the voice of experience. "Secret Service underfoot and the Base Police on alert. Having the president come to a base requires a lot more that just rolling out the red carpet."

The Protestant Chapel was empty and Shalinn wanted to stop. Rose took the tour guide and read as they walked along. "It was dedicated in December 1942. The stained glass windows portray the history of the Marine Corps from 1775 to World War II. Katherine Lamb Tait designed them. The glass came from the U.S., England, France, and Germany. The windows depict Old Testament Archangels above illustrations of major events in Marine Corps history."

Shalinn pointed to one window, "There's the Star of David and the Star of Bethlehem."

"Those are woven into each window," Rose explained. "Both the Jewish and Protestant use this Chapel."

They drove out Sneads Ferry Road to a protected wildlife habitat. Getting out of the car, they took a short walk.

"The brochure notes that Camp Lejeune has one of the healthiest populations of the endangered red-cockaded woodpecker in the southeastern United States." 'They carve out nests in live trees and the resin from the pine tree protects the babies from snakes and other predators.'

"Bill dear, with all that has been going on I feel a little tired," Shalinn admitted. "I think I have seen enough. Why don't we go back to the hotel? Maybe this evening we can go out to dinner somewhere."

"Mom, that's fine with us," Dennis agreed. "We can take you back and then I can run Rose home."

The red flags were flying at Poggemeyer's Peak, a live fire training area for automatic weapons, grenade launchers, and fifty-caliber machine guns.

Rose and Shalinn jumped at the sound of the rat-a-tat-tat machine gun fire that could be heard over the engine and air-conditioning noise.

"I am so happy that you will be coming back to Nashville with us for a few days." Shalinn patted Rose's arm. "Do you know what you will do now?

"I'll continue at the café," supplied Rose. "I have a home here and with Gunny hiring a new waitress my work will be a lot lighter. We want to expand our evening menu and try to draw in more customers. Gunny is also thinking about a Sunday buffet."

"I hope everything works out for you Rose, but if it doesn't, I want your promise that you'll call and let us know."

"It will all work out," she assured Shalinn. "It will just take time, but I promise that if it doesn't I'll call."

Dennis dropped his parents off at the hotel, setting a pickup time for seven o'clock.

"Dennis," she paused, trying to find the words. "I'm sorry about the mess this morning." She watched his mouth pucker with just a glimpse of his tongue showing and he started to chuckle. She was reminded of the kiss they shared a couple of days earlier and felt her blood heat. His laughter brought her back to reality. "What's so funny?"

"Is that what has had you as tight as a fiddle all day?" He subdued his mirth and observed from his peripheral vision the slight frown. "I'm sorry Rose, that was insensitive of me. He won't touch you as long as I'm around, and Dad and I will make sure he doesn't after all this is over."

She had one of those "Yeah, right, when pigs can fly," looks of doubt.

"What shall we do for lunch?" He changed the subject. "It's a long time 'til we pick up Mom and Dad."

"Let's go back to the Café. I know the cook and can sweet talk him out of a meal anytime." She put on a big smile despite the feelings of apprehension that seeing Richard had caused.

Pulling into a parking spot Rose was the first out of the car. "Go and grab a spot, I need to run upstairs for one minute and then I'll show you how to sweet talk a crusty old Gunny out of a couple of meals."

The whole café jumped with a start when the door marked with a Private Entrance sign exploded open. Before Dennis could stand, she had stormed across the room. The muscles in her neck were extended, her face red and contorted with rage.

"I'll kill that son-of-a-bitch with my own bare hands!"

# Chapter Nine

"You said he wouldn't touch me!" She slammed both hands palm first on the table. "The only thing you did was take me away from here so I couldn't protect what was mine!"

"Rose!" Gunny barked over her yelling.

"You want to know what's wrong? Why don't you go upstairs and see what I'm yelling about?" She forcefully pointed towards the stairs.

Gunny beat Dennis to the door only because he was closest. They both took the steps two at a time and came to an abrupt halt at the door. The place was a shambles. Someone, and Dennis didn't have to guess who, had meticulously searched the apartment. What little Rose had, was scattered across the floor. The couch was shredded along with the overstuffed chair. Being careful not to disturb anything, he stepped into the room.

"Gunny, call the police," he ordered. "Keep everyone out."

In the bedroom, it was worse. Dennis wasn't a man to show much emotion but he felt his heart breaking over this wanton destruction of Rose's things. He backed out of the room, stepping over the now shredded remains of what had been Rose's wedding dress.

The police arrived and began their investigation. The lock on the back door showed signs of being tampered with. The evidence van arrived and the team was soon lifting prints from the room.

Rose was so weary from answering the same questions over again and again. Yes, she had money in the apartment, approximately fifty dollars. Yes, both doors were locked. No, this was the first time she had seen her father in four years. No, she had no idea where he could have gone.

Dennis gave an accurate description of Richard and what he was wearing to the detective.

"Mrs. Grady, the evidence technician is done. Would you mind going through your things to see if anything is missing?" requested the Detective.

Standing in the door of the apartment, she felt the overwhelming despair of the destruction and the violation of her privacy. Leaning on Dennis she stepped over the debris on the floor. Gravitating toward the remains of the couch the coffee table was suspiciously free of objects. "My picture of Mark is gone. The one he sent the day before he was killed."

Dennis wondered how she held up through everything. He felt the despair weigh heavily on his soul.

"The money is gone," her voice emotionless. The bathroom was a shambles, toilet paper everywhere, perfume and lotions dumped on the floor. She went into her bedroom and shuddered. All the clothes she had just bought were destroyed. Looking around she noticed the white fabric of her wedding dress crumpled on the floor, now nothing more than rags. She buried her face in Dennis's shoulder and wept.

"Mrs. Grady," the detective inquired. "I know this is difficult for you. Is anything else missing; credit cards, checks, I.D., anything he might be able to use against you?"

"The check book." Turning from Dennis's comforting embrace, she rummaged through the debris on the floor. She turned her head and saw Dennis on his hands and knees shifting through the pile.

The detective and two other police officers were soon on the floor searching.

Sitting in the middle of the room, she hung her head. Closing off the world that had literally been turned upside down, she reached down and drew strength from a mother's love and Mark's tender care. From the difficulty and trials of her past she donned her armor. Standing she declared. "It's gone."

Dennis watched the transformation. He had seen it before. One moment a soldier was cowering in the mud, the next he was leading the charge through a barrage of enemy fire.

"Mrs. Grady, we're through here. If we have any more questions or find anything we'll be in touch," the officer informed her.

"Come on Rose." Taking her hand Dennis gently pulled her towards him. "I'll call Mother and then we are going shopping."

"I have to clean this place and I don't have a checkbook," she reminded him.

"Don't worry about this mess Rose," Gunny told her. "I'll have it squared away before you get back."

"I'll take care of the expense." Dennis saw the flare of defiance in her eyes. "No arguments allowed. If you insist, you can pay me back but we are going shopping. Right Gunny?"

"Right," he agreed.

Ten minutes later, Dennis ushered Rose into Belks while he made a phone call.

"Dad, afraid we won't be able to make dinner tonight. Shawnassy came back while we were at the base and destroyed her apartment."

"Everything, nothing was left."

"He forced the back door. Sloppy job but effective."

"You're right Dad, I was thinking about calling the Ferret."

"Good idea. I'll call both of them and get them on the next plane."

Dennis hung up and called the Nashville office.

She was finishing the last of her purchases at Belk's when Dennis came back. They took the packages to the car and started visiting the other stores that Rose had been to. She groaned inwardly with each purchase mentally adding up the growing debt, as Dennis handed the cashier the plastic card.

They ate at the mall, the last of the packages filling a chair and piled on the floor.

"I think you should stay somewhere else tonight, Rose, "he suggested.

Rose returned his no-nonsense glare and tone of voice. "No."

"It may not be safe," he tried to reason with her. "He might come back." Dennis watched her face take on an evil grin.

"I hope he does," she threatened.

The ice that dripped off her words sent a forbidding chill through his veins. He wasn't sure whom he was trying to protect from whom. "You could get hurt."

"My mother lived in fear of that—," She tried to find a less harsh word and failed. "That bastard 'til the day she died. He knew it and exploited that knowledge constantly."

"Will you stay at Gunny's place tonight? Please." Dennis gave her his most beguiling smile.

"Nice try Dennis." She countered with a smile of her own.

Her smile slammed into him and chipped away at his resolve. "Okay, you win. I'll talk to Gunny and see if I can stay in the room next to yours. There is another apartment right."

"Yes, but it's used for storage and unfinished." She tried to forestall his decision.

"I ah, think I can survive." Dennis winked and again gave her a cultivated smile that had been so effective in the past.

This teasing and bantering was a reminder of Mark. It brought back the heartache of her loss and at the same time a reason to smile. She would enjoy his company while he was here, if nothing more than to relieve the pain of their shared loss.

When they returned to the apartment, it had been swept. Even the black smudges from the police evidence technicians had been wiped clean. The couch was covered with a spread and the chair was gone.

Gunny came over and helped carry the mountain of clothes upstairs. "I swear girl you're bringing home more clothes than I threw away."

"Thank you Gunny for cleaning this mess." She gave him a hug and a kiss on the cheek. "Dennis wants to stay in the other apartment tonight. Just in case."

"Not a bad idea," he agreed. "The door is unlocked, never had a reason to lock it."

Dennis opened the door and flipped the light switch. In the middle of the floor sat an empty bottle of whiskey. Next to the bottle was the picture, now ripped in half. To think that Richard had hidden in here while the police were right next-door was shedding new insight on his character. Not only was he mean and vengeful but calculating as well. Probably slipping out well after everyone had gone and leaving behind a message of his presence.

"Mighty sure of himself isn't he?" Gunny noticed the bottle.

"He's a cocky rat," Dennis muttered. "For a rat you need a rat catcher and I have one of the best in the business. He'll be here at midnight.

"Stick around for a while Gunny I'll run over to the motel and pack." He went down the stairs.

A knock on the door brought Gunny to the street entrance.

"I am looking for Rose Grady."

A well-dressed man stood at the door. He was broad shouldered medium build, not much over her own height. His black wavy hair was turning gray at the temples. Somewhere in the back corner of her memory, his face emerged from the fog of her early childhood.

"I'm sorry." Gunny blocked the door. "Rose has had a hard day and is going to have another difficult one tomorrow."

"Rose Grady," he addressed her over Gunny's shoulder. "May I speak with you a moment? In private."

"Is this about my husband?"

"No. This is about Richard.

"Who are you?" She demanded walking down the stairs.

He opened his billfold.

Rose looked at his identification. 'Rodgers, Thomas D. Central Intelligence' "What's this got to do with me?

"Relax Rose," Rodgers said. "We just want to find him before the local police or the FBI does."

"Mark's brother will be back in a few minutes. You can wait upstairs."

"I would rather this be private," he stated.

"It's with Dennis, or not at all." She held his gaze and didn't back down.

A short while later a figure moved stealthily through the shadows and up the stairs.

"Jeess, Dennis don't sneak up on an old man like that," Gunny admonished. "I must be slipping. I didn't hear a sound."

"If you'd heard me, I would be the one that was slipping," Dennis stated.

He pulled up short when he noticed the stranger in Rose's apartment.

"Dennis." Gunny made the introduction. "This is Agent Rodgers with the CIA."

Rodgers offered his hand to Dennis.

When it was refused coldly, he sneered. "You don't have much love for the agency, do you Grady?"

"Should I?" he asked. "After what I saw of your operations in Laos and Vietnam?" Rodgers was honest enough that he looked uncomfortable with the memories.

"We did what we had to do." His attempt to justify the agencies actions was ignored.

"That still didn't make it right." Dennis glared at Rodgers.

"You said you wanted to talk." Rose tried to defuse the tension.

"We feel that Richard may show up here soon," Rodgers stated. "Your man may be able to get close to him."

"My man," Dennis feigned surprise and confusion.

"Come on Grady," he admonished. "Even if we can't be friends, at least let's be professional here. You know I'm talking about Frank so stop with the games."

Rose watched the verbal sparring play out like two fighters circling, testing each other's abilities.

Rose felt the contempt Dennis had, not for Rodgers personally but for the agency he represented.

"Just what is the purpose of this visit?" grilled Dennis. "Why is the glorious CIA trying to find a homeless drunk?"

"Richard's dependence on booze and gambling is what got him in trouble," Rodgers explained. "His past is something we do not wish to, shall we say, be brought out for public scrutiny or sold to the highest bidder."

"You're saying that Richard is a national security risk." Rose was finding all this a little too incredible to be real.

Her eyes danced with suppressed laughter, the corners of her mouth twitched. Dennis observed the moment reality set in when Rodgers spoke in a cold deadly hush.

"Yes, Mrs. Grady. That is precisely what I am saying. He knows people, places and dates that would not only be an embarrassment for the agency, but would undermine its operations and do harm to our country's diplomatic relationships with other countries. Four years ago, he stole a highly sensitive document. We have never recovered it, and believe me, we looked. After we arrested him, we turned his trailer apart. We never found the document or you. We feel that is one reason he may show up here. There is a possibility that you may have it, or had it at one time, and not realized it."

"So now, you want Richard to be just dumped into your lap, when he shows up here again." Dennis toyed with a pen. "What guarantee do I have that within, say two, three years, you no longer consider him a risk and let him out of your '*hospital*'."

"You have my word."

Rose shuddered inwardly at the implication of what wasn't said but revealed by the tone of his voice. An unstoppable gasp escaped her lips.

"Agent Rodgers, my father has already been here and gone and I hope I never see him again. He trashed my apartment, stole my checks, and all the cash I had in the house."

"When was he here? Was there anything else taken? Did you have anything that you brought from Florida?" he rattled off the questions non-stop.

"He was here this morning and came back this afternoon. That's when he trashed the apartment, and nothing else was taken except a photo of Mark that she had received in the mail," Dennis answered.

"Anything else?" Rodgers asked.

"No," Rose whispered.

"Rose, I'm going to try to make this a little easier for you." Rodgers paused, trying to find the right way to break this information to her.

Rose waited, watching the emotions play across his face.

"Richard," he continued, "is not your father, that is not your natural father."

"If Carmen were alive she would have to agree with you. He wasn't much of a husband…"

"Rose," he interrupted. "You don't understand. Twenty years ago, he was part of an operation that went wrong. Somehow, we were compromised and walked into a trap. Of the group that went in only two came out, both wounded. Richard's injuries left him sterile."

The impact of Rodgers' statement was a slap in the face. Yet, at the same time she felt a heavy weight being lifted from her soul.

"You're sure?" Dennis sought more assurance.

"Rodgers nodded, his face drawn as if he was reliving a painful nightmare.

"I was the other survivor," he revealed. "We were in the same hospital room. I was there when the doctors told Richard the news. Richard changed after that, started drinking; beating on your mother like it was her fault or something. Carmen was a wonderful person, Rose; she didn't deserve to be treated like that. No woman does."

Rodgers eyes softened with the mention of her mother's name. Some inner sense revealed more than just a casual friendship between the two.

"You loved Carmen," she declared. "Yet you left her in that situation. Why?" Rose asked, not really sure she wanted the answer.

"I was already married. We didn't intend on having these feelings. They just happened. Many times in the hospital when she would come to visit, Richard would be asleep or in therapy. She would visit with me, sometimes for hours. My wife was in a different state and couldn't get down very often because of her health."

"After Richard got out of the hospital, Carmen turned to me for help. I tried to talk to him but it only made it worse. He moved Carman and you to Florida when you were six."

"This is all rather sudden, I hope you don't expect me to jump up and give you a big hug and call you Daddy? Beside we always lived in Florida."

Rodgers took out an envelope and handed it to Rose.

"You always lived near the ocean," Rodgers corrected. "You were born in Norfolk Virginia and lived just off the beach the first few years. You were too young to remember. If it helps any, I'm sorry."

She opened the envelope and took out several pictures of Carmen and her when she was a baby. When she was older and Carmen was holding her next to the entrance to the Norfolk Naval base. Still others taken at different stages of her life while living in Florida, many she suspected of being shot with a telephoto lens.

"I'm afraid that the statute of limitations has expired for an apology." She stood on trembling legs, and walked across the floor. She stared unseeing out the window, thinking about what Rodgers had just told her.

All those years of lies, the wasted years of living with a man who was not the father of her child, the heartache her mother must have borne in silence. Knowing she couldn't be with the man she loved, and the man she was with didn't love her or her child.

Agent Rodgers quietly left but not without turning back as he reached the door. "Rose, for what it's worth, I am proud of the way you turned out."

"You okay?" Dennis asked.

"No, I am not okay. That's the most stupid question you could ask right now."

"Rose I know you're angry but..."

"Angry, is that what you think I am. For eighteen years, I have been lied to, beaten, and slapped around by a man pretending to be my father. Pretending to care about us. I've watched my mother cower before him in fear and hide in our miserable trailer for days 'til the bruises faded enough she could go back to work, and you have the damned audacity to think I'm angry."

She shook off his hand. "I don't want or need your sympathy right now," she lied. "Just put that bastard, no I'm the bastard or is an illegitimate girl a bitch. It's really complicated now to know who or what I am. Just put him where he belongs."

Going to her bedroom, Rose prayed he would leave. When he did, the rest of her was disappointed. She kept telling herself that turning to Dennis for comfort would just be opening her heart to more heartache. In time, the hole left there would be filled with caring for Mark's child. That had to be enough. She was glad that Richard was not her real father. There would be no sympathy or hard feelings when he was put away.

Rose stared into the bathroom mirror. Funny the face in the mirror was the same one as yesterday and the day before. The odd colored hair that ran in her family, and then only on the girls' side. The eyes that went with the hair, a shade of green of such intensity that as a child she had been self-conscious, wanting to wear sunglasses where ever she went.

Rose Ann Rodgers, the name had a nice ring to it but it didn't fit the face in the mirror. Rose Ann Shawnassy stared back. Only now, it was Grady. She had a splitting headache and wondered if the face in the mirror was suffering too. "Rose Ann Shawnassy Rodgers Grady," she laughed. Sounded like one of those prissy aristocrats names. If her mother had just had the courage to go after the man she loved, and who obviously loved her.

She tried a smile for the image in the mirror. The mouth smiled back but the eyes didn't reflect any outward change. Brushing her hair, Rose tried to sort out her feelings. Finding emptiness and confusion she pushed the conversation into the far reaches of her mind. When she had time, she would examine them more closely.

* * * * *

"I'm going to bed then." Gunny started down the steps.

Dennis made sure the front door and the café access door were locked. Dressed in dull black he sat unnoticed in the doorway. Rose came into the living room and looked around, flipped a switch. An exhaust fan in the ceiling started. He would have to rely on sight and a sense of presence. She was wearing a sheer robe with nothing underneath. Rose turned the light off, plunging the room into semi-darkness. The sight of her was throwing off his concentration.

"Rose, don't turn on the light. I can't take the chance he might be across the street watching through a window," he whispered.

"Damn you Grady," she muttered. "Have you been out there since Gunny left?"

"Go to bed Rose." He whispered just loud enough for her to hear.

It was after midnight when Dennis slipped unnoticed into the night. Within minutes, two silent figures stepped out of the shadows and joined him.

"Find anything?" Dennis asked.

"Some, maybe more important is what I didn't find," the Ferret acknowledge. "Other than a couple reports of domestic violence that's it. Records are sealed. Barney couldn't even get to them."

"We had an interesting visit this evening from the CIA," Dennis informed them. "An Agent Rodgers. Seems our man Richard has been spending time for espionage and has recently escaped. They think Rose might have what they are looking for," he paused. "Frank, you're prior CIA. You ever heard of Rodgers?"

"Yeah, I know him," Frank admitted. "Hell of a good guy. He and I go all the way back to Cuba and the missile crisis. We were both young and ready to get to the field. We learned quick or died in those days. We had orders to kill Castro, then all of a sudden the orders were cancelled and we had to find our own way back to the extraction point."

"Stay on your toes. This one is slippery. He stayed in the apartment across the hall while the police were there." Dennis turned and vanished into the shadows. He checked the spare apartment and found it secure. With the windows closed, it was suffocating in the room. He crossed the hallway and like a ghost, entered Rose's living room. Probing the darkened corners of the room, he verified that he was alone.

She lay on the bed, the sheet tossed aside. The dim light from the streetlights and neon signs danced across her pale flesh. The sound of her breathing with the rise and fall of her breasts kicked his heart into overdrive. The heat of his desire settled below the waist. He backed out of the room, found a dark corner, and settled in for the remainder of the night.

In the early morning hours, he felt the vibration as her feet hit the floor. Dennis stilled his breathing as she walked within mere inches of where he sat. He felt himself respond when the breeze carried her musky scent to him. When the shower came on, he slipped out the door and once again took up his post at the head of the stairs. The sounds of Gunny working in the kitchen drifted up to him.

The thought of Rose in the shower all slick and soapy was doing disastrous things to his thoughts and concentration. He couldn't afford the luxury of daydreaming about something that couldn't be.

Rose finished her shower and wrapped a large towel around her. "You can use the bath now." She spoke as she entered the bedroom and closed the door.

"Stay in your room 'til I'm done Rose," he instructed through the closed door.

He wasn't taking any chances with her safety. Leaving the door open in order to view her door, he stripped and stepped into the shower.

Rose fumed; she had things to do and couldn't do them stuck in her room like some disobedient child. She opened the door and stopped. Dennis was in the shower, curtain open and she had a full view of his lithe frame. Across the distance, she saw clearly the puckered scars of past injuries. Her eyes traveled downward of their own accord until she was openly staring at his manhood protruding like a tree from a forest of dark tangled hair.

"You could've closed the door," she snapped.

"You could've stayed in the room like I asked. Rose, if you're in the other room and Richard comes back I won't know it until it's too late."

"This is ridiculous." She turned and closed the door behind her. Leaning with her head against the door, she replayed his image in her mind. Feeling herself turn moist at the thought of his being in her shower as if waiting for her to join him, Rose forced her thoughts away from Dennis to the day ahead.

# Chapter Ten

Dennis and Rose were seated at a table when William Sr. and Shalinn entered and shook the water off their umbrellas before joining them at the table.

"Rose, my dear," Shalinn gave her a comforting hug before she sat down. "What you have been through, I am so sorry for what happened. Did you get everything you needed or do we need to go shopping this morning?"

"Thanks to Dennis," she said graciously, "I have everything I need 'til I start back to work. By then, I'll have my new checks. Which reminds me, Dennis, I've got to contact the bank this morning first thing."

Dennis watched a beggar emerge from the shadows and cross the street. He entered the café, sat at the counter, and ordered coffee. With enough volume to reach Dennis's ear he said. "Nothing else, just coffee."

The waitress came over and they ordered.

The Ferret drank his coffee, laid the money on the counter, and as unnoticed as he had entered, stepped into the rainy day to continue his search.

They were just finishing their meal when a man entered wearing a pair of non-descriptive coveralls and asked to speak privately with the owner. A few minutes later, he set to work installing a state-of-the-art security system in the café and the living area above.

They left and headed towards the base. Shalinn held her hand giving her the assurance that she wasn't alone.

Somehow, it wasn't the same as holding his. Strangely for all her independence, she was coming to rely on Dennis for too many things. This had to stop. In a few days, he would be just a memory.

Dennis fell in line at the gate. The guards were slowly checking names against a roster of family members. They were waved through the gate and told to "follow the signs." Dennis pulled into the parking area reserved for family members and again was checked by a marine sentry.

Dennis took her hand as they got out and started across the lawn to the pavilion behind the Second Division Headquarters building. "After tomorrow," she whispered to her heart. Right now, his touch, his nearness, was her strength.

The rain was cold and in spite of the umbrella Dennis held, the rain found its way down her neck causing a shiver that once started, didn't want to end. The dismal rain drenched the sweeping lawn soaking her shoes and seeped in to make things that much more miserable. The curtain of rain and the low hanging clouds had reduced the visibility obscuring most of the wide waters of New River.

Rose drew strength and warmth from Dennis's arm that held her close. She couldn't help but notice the rank and file of marines already standing on the lawn, seemingly oblivious to the conditions around them.

The flags of five nations hung heavily from their poles. The dignitaries arrived, Ambassadors from Great Britain, France, Italy, and Lebanon. Marine officers from Camp Lejeune and Washington along with the navy chaplains. The band from the Marine Second Division was off to the side. All waited for the commander in chief, the president of the United States.

A reverberate hush enveloped the already quiet crowd as ten servicemen, wounded twelve days prior in Lebanon, were escorted in wheelchairs to the front of those assembled. A thunderous round of applause erupted for those that had endured the horrifying events that had not only shocked the nation but the world. The applause died, and Rose watched President and Mrs. Reagan approach.

Mrs. Reagan shielded the president with a clear plastic umbrella from the drenching rain. She could not shield him, her husband, and the leader of the free world, from the pain and anguish that Rose saw etched on his face. Instead of going to the front with the other dignitaries, President Reagan walked determinedly over to those ten who were confined in wheelchairs. Stopping in front of each man, he shook his hand. Reaching the last man he slowly stood, as if weighted down by each man's pain and suffering.

The national anthem for each country represented was played. At the first notes of the "Star Spangled Banner," the crowd already on their feet seemed to stand taller, a little prouder, aware that the price of freedom was all too often paid with blood.

Navy Chaplin Curtis Schmidtlein gave the benediction. Rose bowed her head as her own heart, opened for the first time since her mother's death, echoed the chaplain's prayer.

"Father, we ask that the bereaved be strengthened in our sorrow, and our hearts be calmed..."

She felt Dennis's arm tighten around her as if to say, "I am here for you. I will be your strength, you can lean on me."

Listening to the chaplain read from the Twenty-third Psalm and the Book of Romans, it wasn't his voice she heard. Just for a moment, a few fleeting seconds she was beside her mother. Listening to her sweet voice as she read from the scriptures that she kept hidden in their home.

Navy Chaplin, Commodore John McNamara stood and looked out over the throng of people that covered the soggy terraced lawn.

"The Lord has given us a day to match our mood of anguish and grief. Those men who died, invested their life's blood in the future of America. They believed that beauty, peace, and justice would make their sacrifice worthwhile.

"In the tradition of the Bible, those who fell in Lebanon had truly been the peacemakers who will forever be the sons of God."

General Gray stood and stepped to the podium.

"Mr. President, all military commanders throughout time know that from time to time we must say goodbye to our fellow comrades, this is such a time. Since the tragic morning of the bombing, we have received hundreds of messages from around the world. The messages carry two themes.

"The messages we have received, I deem important now. They say, 'General, tell the parents, loved ones and friends of our grief. Tell your marines and sailors we share their grief, that we understand, that we have compassion.'

"The second theme that these messages convey, 'This nation wants marines, sailors, soldiers, airmen and Coast

Guard to "Hang Tough". That it is high time we stood up and got counted Mr. President.'"

The general paused, briefly closed his grief-heavy eyes, and then continued, "Make sure that the marines and sailors of the Carolinas stand ready to do whatever needs to be done. And indeed they are."

Lifting his head toward heaven as if to address those who had fallen, "So I say now, our final farewell to our fallen heroes. I want to simply tell them that we will always stand by your families and loved ones. That's the way we are. We will always remember and cherish your courage and your grief."

"The president would like to meet with the family members privately. We have an area out of this rain for you to meet. If you would please go there, the president will be with you shortly."

When President Reagan arrived there was with no fanfare or waving of flags. No band played Hail to the Chief. He walked through the gathered family members shaking hands, his eyes, rimmed with unshed tears. His face etched with their shared grief. Standing before the group of mothers, fathers, wives, and children, he spoke movingly and with deep compassion.

"No words can make things easier," he paused. "I ask myself, where do we find men like these? We all know the answer: they come from families like yours. From farms and villages, towns and cities across this great nation. What they died for, us, our country, is what America is all about."

Rose walked back to the car leaning heavily on Dennis, thankful for his support and strength. Tears that had been held at bay now trickled slowly down her checks.

Shalinn came and drew her into an embrace.

"Oh Rose." She whispered brokenly as their tears mingled. "He's gone. My boy is gone."

Wordlessly Dennis drew Shalinn and Rose into the circle of his arms.

Bill joined the circle sheltering the women from the storm and from the watching eyes of those around them.

The ride back to Gunny's was a somber one. Rose leaned her head back against the seat, physically and emotionally exhausted.

"Dennis, your mother and I will meet you at the airport," Bill quietly suggested. "Let her," he motioned towards Rose with a shift of his eyes, "get a little sleep before we leave."

Up in her apartment Rose sank wearily onto the couch. The blanket now covering it a staunch reminder at to the state of upheaval her life was in. She turned to Dennis and silently pleaded for his nearness.

A look of compassion spread across his face as he sat down beside her. Sighing as her head found his solid shoulder, she breathed in the freshness of the outdoors. The faint tangy odor of pine mixed with the smell of leather.

Dennis felt the sigh against his neck as he drew his arm around her. Her arm lay across his waist, directly on top of a portion of his body that, despite his best efforts responded to the physical contact. Her breathing deepened in sleep as his quickened to her nearness. Fighting the feelings that were growing, he laid his head back on the couch and closed his eyes only to dream of being surrounded by crimson tongues of fire midst a sea of molten jade.

Dennis opened his eyes to see Gunny standing near the couch. So real was the dream, that he hadn't heard him come in.

"If you are going to make the plane on time," Gunny advised. "You had better get moving."

He woke Rose. Leaving her to freshen up, he went down stairs. "What?" he asked noticing Gunny's hostile expression.

"I just don't want to see Rose get hurt anymore."

"And you think I would hurt her?" Dennis questioned in amazement.

"Not intentionally." Gunny ran his hand tiredly over his face.

The look he received from Gunny spoke volumes that made further words unnecessary.

Rose entered, stopping any more conversation.

She gave Gunny a hug, picked up her small suitcase and handbag, and left the café. Giving the suitcase to Dennis, she watched him stow it in the trunk. They were meeting his parents at the airport in half-an-hour.

"What's troubling you, Rose?" he probed softly. She sat dejectedly, staring out the window. Worry lines creasing smooth creamy skin of her forehead.

"All this expense," she sighed. "It would have been cheaper for me to drive. I already owe you for all the clothes and now for this flight."

"Is it the money or the actual flying that bothers you?" he questioned.

"Both." She turned in her seat to face him. "I have never flown before. All these expenses are eating into my savings. Maybe I should just stay here. Let your family bury Mark in peace. I loved him and I know he loved me and all the services in the world won't bring him back or make his death any easier."

"Mother and Dad would be very hurt if you weren't there," he assured her. "As for the expense, I told you not to worry about it. Besides you have the insurance money to fall back on."

Dennis watched, amazed at the quick transformation her face went through. One moment a docile lamb, dejected, the next there was fire in her eyes making the gold even that much more dominate.

"That money," she bristled. "Is not mine, that's for our child's education. I won't touch that. I don't think Mark would want me to waste that on unnecessary things."

Dennis sat back and adjusted his strategy.

"Rose you just said 'let the family bury Mark'. We can't do that without you there. You are part of our family now."

At this declaration, Rose slumped wearily in the seat. Dennis was fighting dirty and he had just hit below the belt. Family, something she had very little knowledge of, and what she longed the most for…a place to belong. The restaurant was the closest thing she had ever known to belonging to a family. It was a place where she could belong and feel needed. Yet she knew it was but a poor substitute for a real family, surrounded by love and compassion.

"You have that information Commander Rosenthal gave you at the café," Dennis asked.

"Yeah. Why?"

They pulled into the rental return parking lot and turned in the key.

"Show me the papers she gave you," demanded Dennis.

"Why now?"

"Don't argue. I want to see if something I remembered is in there. Please."

"Oh all right." She handed him the envelope and sat down in one of the available chairs.

Dennis found what he was looking for. "See this? This is a travel form. When you get back to Jacksonville, have the Commander help you fill these out and they will reimburse you for your travel expense. I don't want to hear any more about money. Okay?"

After checking in with the Airlines, they found Bill and Shalinn.

Dennis was seated next to Rose in the plane. When the plane started down the runway, he noticed that she had a death grip on the arms of the seat. "Relax, Rose. Everything will be fine." He patted her hand, which she instantly clung to.

"Thank you." She breathed as the aircraft gained altitude. She loosened her grip on his hand, feeling a bit of loss when she let go. "I feel so foolish being frightened but I am."

"Rose, everyone feels frightened occasionally. A person can either control it or the fear will control them." He thoughtfully studied her face for several minutes. "You are remarkable in your ability to overcome your fears."

"Ha, that's a joke," she scoffed. "First time I saw you I ran and hid. That sure sounds like control."

"You're here beside me," he reasoned. "You stood up to your dad and actually slapped him. Although he probably deserved it, I'm not sure it was a good idea. You faced life on the street and survived. If you hadn't fallen on a knife, you would've been back to work immediately. I think you are a remarkable woman."

He watched as she suppressed a laugh. "You find that funny?"

"Is there any Irish in your family?" she giggled.

"Why do you ask?" he smiled.

"Because somewhere along the way," she laughed. "You and Mark both kissed the same blarney stone."

Dennis watched as the laugh lines disappeared as she became serious. The eyes lost the sparkle, her mouth no longer had the turned up corners.

"I appreciate all that you have done and are still doing in regards to Richard. When you came out to Jacksonville you started asking questions. You didn't figure I would find out, did you? One of the girls overheard you…"

"And she told you," he finished for her.

"When did I change from being a conniving little tramp that you had to investigate to a remarkable woman? That's why when this is over and done with you will get your money back for all the clothes as well as this trip." She looked out the window at the checkerboard pattern of the land far below as it played peek-a-boo with the clouds.

*Damn. Here I thought I was making headway and she broadsides me.*

"I don't know when I changed my mind about you Rose—but I did."

"Thanks for the change of heart." She leaned her head back and closed her eyes. "Now all that's left is to figure out those times that you were warm, understanding and caring. Were they because you were still checking up on me, you felt pity or did you change your mind that quickly?"

How could he answer that question when he wasn't even sure himself.

"You know Dennis," she whispered. "When you find that special woman in your life, I hope she can tolerate your suspicious nature because, quite frankly, at times, it is suffocating."

Propping his elbow on the seat arm, Dennis rested his head in his hand. She had opened her defense, allowed him to get in close, and then closed the door. Everything she said had been true.

The plane landed at Raleigh to take on passengers. Rose sat trying to appear relaxed in her chair. She fought the sickening feeling, refusing to take Dennis's hand that was only inches away from hers.

The first thing upon landing in Nashville, Rose went to the bathroom and heaved. Obviously there was someone else who wasn't comfortable with flying.

"We live about twelve miles from the airport, right on the Cumberland," Shalinn said with pride. "I just love the quiet neighborhood and the boats on the water, it is just so peaceful."

They were soon on Interstate 40 headed east. Taking an exit ramp, within a couple of miles Bill was entering an area of fewer houses. He pulled in at a gorgeous two-story brick home.

"Well," Shalinn asked. Her hand swept along the flowerbeds and manicured lawn. A pool glistened in the back yard. "Here we are. What do you think?"

"What do I think," she mimicked. "I think it's beautiful beyond words. You must be very happy." Rose felt as out of place as Cinderella at the ball. This wasn't her world and what's more, she felt that this wasn't Mark's world.

"Somehow," she voiced her thoughts. "I just can't see Mark growing up in a place like this."

Shalinn laughed, "Oh, my goodness sakes, no. We bounced around all over the world living in military housing and rentals for twenty-five years. It's just been since Bill retired that we have lived here. His security business has grown beyond our dreams. Now that Dennis is helping, Bill can stay at home more. I like having him around, most of the time."

The foyer was open with a curving staircase to the second floor. An exquisite chandelier hung from the ceiling. Off to one side was a large kitchen with oak cabinets. Shinny copper bottomed pans hung from a rack over the stove centered in the room. Countertop space was abundant and the recessed lighting provided ample light anywhere in the kitchen. An oak table and benches provided a cozy place to have morning coffee while visiting with friends or for a family meal.

The formal dinning room had a walnut table and matching china cabinet. The sunken living room, with its sectional sofa and Lazy-boy recliner overlooked the patio, pool, and the river beyond. Shalinn showed her the master bedroom with a plush carpet and a huge king-size bed with its rich cherry wood headboard. The master bath was a luxury, a sunken tub, and large walk-in double shower. An opaque glass wall allowed soft light to filter into the room.

The upstairs had four bedrooms, each with its own view of the river. Two full baths completed the upstairs. Two of the rooms lacked any personality, looking like they had been photocopied right out of the Better Homes & Garden fashion pages.

She spotted Dennis's room instantly. The hairbrush and cologne set off to the side, a pair of Western Boots that were placed by the dresser. The last room was Mark's; she felt the tears come of their own free will. Picking up a school football picture, she traced his outline on the glass. The trophy on the dresser was inscribed, 'Mark Grady, Nineteen Seventy-Seven, Most Valuable Player.'

Shalinn came to her, tears in her own eyes they held each other and grieved over their loss. "Rose dear, I think Mark would want you to stay here. I know eventually we both have to let go, but for now—you rest for a little while then we will go to the funeral home later."

She wandered around the spacious home and found her way to the patio. The tranquil water of the pool looked inviting. Sticking her hand in the pool and splashing the water, she was pleasantly surprised to find it warm. Watching the ripples spread out across the surface of the pool, she reflected that her life was like that, tranquil and serene, until Mark had come along and stirred the surface of her existence with his love. The atmosphere was so quiet it lulled her to sleep.

"Rose," Dennis called softly. "Rose, wake up. It's time to go."

She sat up, forgetting for a moment where she was. "Sorry, I must have fallen asleep. It's so peaceful out here."

"Mother says we need to be going. I brought you a sweater, it's starting to get cool."

Rose sat in the funeral home; a sea of faces swam before her. Most were clients of the family business or its employees. City Officials came because of where Mark had died. The closed casket was a constant reminder of the violent way he died. Through the short time they were there, she made all the proper responses to the people's expressions of sympathy. People who never knew that Mark was warm and caring, didn't know that he liked marshmallow malts and long walks barefoot on the beach. Even his family didn't know that he wanted to make a career of the corps.

Nevertheless, she did. Rose knew the tender caress of his hands, the passion of his loving, the strength of his arms as he held her close. The tender caress and the shelter within his arms were gone…now, only a memory. She was left with the sweet seed of his passion growing within. She might never be able to give her child the wealth of Mark's family; the fancy home on the river or the private schools but the child would have love. In the end, that was the most important.

# Chapter Eleven

Dennis turned the news on when they got home from the funeral home.

"Earlier this morning President Reagan attended a memorial service at Camp Lejeune honoring the dead and wounded marines from Lebanon and Grenada. Before boarding Air Force One to return to Washington the president had these comments."

"Officers and men and women of the corps, ladies and gentlemen, I came here today to pay homage to the heroes of Lebanon and Grenada. We grieve along with the families of these brave, proud Americans who have given their lives for their country and for the preservation of peace.

"I have just met with the families of many of those who were killed. I think all Americans would cradle them in our arms if we could. We share their sorrow. I want all of you who lost loved ones and friends to know that the thoughts and prayers of this nation are with you.

"If this country is to remain a force for good in the world, we'll face times like these, times of sadness and loss. Your fellow citizens know and appreciate that marines and their families are carrying a heavy burden.

"America seeks no new territory, nor do we wish to dominate others. We commit our resources and risk the lives of those in our armed forces to rescue others from bloodshed and turmoil, and to prevent humankind from drowning in a sea of tyranny.

"The world looks to America for leadership. And America looks to the men in its armed forces... to the Corps of Marines, to the Navy, the Army.

"Freedom is being tested throughout the world.

"In spite of the complexity and special hardships of the Lebanese crisis, we have stood firm. As ever, leathernecks are willing to accept their mission and do their duty. This honest patriotism and dedication to duty overwhelms the rest of us.

"In a free society there's bound to be disagreement about any decisive course of action. Some of those so quick to criticize, I invite them to read the letters I've received. Marines have a saying—"We take care of our own." Well, America, with the help of marines, will take care of our own.

"I came here today to honor so many who did their duty and gave that last, full measure of their devotion. They kept faith with us and our way of life. We wouldn't be free long, but for the dedication of such individuals. They were heroes. We're grateful to have had them with us.

"The motto of the United States Marine Corps: "Semper Fidelis"—always faithful. Well, the rest of us must remain always faithful to those ideals, which so many have given their lives to protect. Our heritage of liberty must be preserved and passed on. Let no terrorist question our will or no tyrant doubt our resolve. Americans have courage and determination, and we must not and will not be intimidated by anyone, anywhere.

"Since 1775, marines, just like many of you, have shaped the strength and resolve of the United States. Your role is as important today as at any time in our history.

"Our hearts go out to the families of the brave men that we honor today. Let us close ranks with them in tribute to our fallen heroes, their loved ones, who gave more than can ever be repaid. They're now part of the soul of this great country and will live as long as our liberty shines as a beacon of hope to all those who long for freedom and a better world.

"One of the men in the early days of our nation, John Stuart Mill, said, 'War is an ugly thing, but not the ugliest of things. The ugliest is that man who thinks nothing is worth fighting or dying for and lets men better and braver than himself protect him.' You are doing that for all of us.

"God bless you and thank you for what you're doing."

Rose was restless, she couldn't sleep. Standing in front of the window, she looked longingly at the pool. She had only been swimming once in all the years since she left home. Mark had taken her to a secluded beach one night and they had gone swimming. She didn't own a suit but the lure of the water was too great. Rose slipped into her robe and crept down the darkened stairs.

Dennis felt more than heard the door close. Going to the window he experienced a pang of envy as Rose slid into the cool water. Unless she had purchased a swimsuit at the first store, she was wearing her lacy panties and bra. The pool lights were low and she looked like a mermaid swimming through the water. He should let her swim in privacy, but like the sailors who drove their ships onto the rocky shores following the siren of the mermaid's song, he was unable to turn aside. Not until Rose had left the pool and entered the house, did he leave the shadows and step away from the window.

The light came on in the bathroom. Only the door separated him. Visualizing her taking off the wet clothes, her skin still damp from her swim, Dennis groaned over the perplexity of his desire for her as a woman and his role as protector. Who would protect Rose from the protector? The morning sky was laced with fiery fingers of crimson and gold before he closed his eyes.

Shalinn lightly tapped on the door and entered. Crossing the room to where Rose sat clasping a picture of Mark to her breast, she gently cuddled her daughter. "Take it home with you dear, Mark would want you to have it."

"Thank you," she whimpered. Tears silently fell tracing a path down her cheeks to drop on the glass surface.

"Breakfast is ready. Please," she urged. "You need to eat."

Setting the picture on the dresser Rose wiped her eyes and followed Shalinn down the stairs.

The sweet aroma of bananas, apples, and cinnamon fresh from the oven greeted her. Bill and Dennis were seated at the kitchen nook, their hands folded around steaming cups of coffee.

She slid in beside Dennis, he looked up, and their eyes met in an unguarded moment of heated desire. Confused that her feelings were being reflected in his eyes, Rose broke the contact. This was Mark's brother. She buttered a slice of bread and ate in silence, consumed with grief, sorrow and an awareness of Dennis that she knew should be avoided.

Shalinn brought out the family albums. Rose felt out-of-place, an interloper that by a quirk of fate had placed her in another world. The birthday parties, the ball games, Christmas in Florida one year and the next in Norfolk, Virginia. In all too many pictures, Bill was absent. An inscription on the bottom told the story of a military family, …on the Saratoga, …on the Kennedy, …in Iceland, or …in Naples, Italy. Then there was the reminder of the secrecy of his work, …Dad's location- Unknown.

These were all someone else's memories. They would never be hers. When Shalinn was a Grandmother, she would share with her child stories about a father they would never know.

"Excuse me, please," she stood. "I'm sorry I can't do this right now. I think I'll take a walk 'til its time to go.

Shalinn took her hand. "Rose dear, I understand. I'll send Dennis to find you when its time to get ready."

Along the riverbank, she scuffed her feet in the sand. Flinging flat rocks to skip across the water. Sitting by the water's edge with her arms wrapped around her legs she gazed despondently at the swirling water that lapped at her feet.

"Rose." Dennis squatted on the balls of his feet next to her. "Rose, Mother says it's time." He stood and held out his hand. For the longest time, he thought she would refuse. Slowly Rose put her hand in his, and he helped her to her feet.

In the depths of his eyes was sympathy. Gone was the desire of the morning, if it had even been there.

Up in her room, she pulled her slacks down and stepped out of them. Adding her blouse and bra to the pile she opened her suitcase and took out the underclothes she was going to wear. "Damn these things."

Dennis knocked and opened the door. Only his quick reflexes kept him from getting a pair of suntan colored nylons in the face. "Cease fire!" Picking up the missile she had fired at the door, he looked first at the nylons and then at her.

"Wrong size, color, or just in the mood to throw something?" The sight of her standing there in nothing but a pair of shear panties sent heated desire pumping through his body.

"Try a snag," she fumed, "as in non-repairable, non-wearable. And the only *damn* pair I own."

"Okay!" Dennis held up his hand in self-defense to her barrage. "I get the picture. We'll stop and get a pair on the way to the service. As soon as you're dressed we can leave." Dennis backed out of the room berating himself for the thoughts that filled his mind.

A few minutes later, Rose came down the stairs looking very elegant in her matching black skirt and jacket. Her hair bounced and shimmered in the reflected light, reminding him of the circle of fire from his dream.

Bill pulled into a convenience store and Rose hopped out. Standing in front of the display case she fidgeted, Large Black, Petite White, Extra Large Tan, Medium Red, and Large Nude.

"Are these all you have?" she asked.

Dennis watched from the car as she slammed a package on the counter and the checkout lady's face had a shocked appearance. Rose stomped out of the store muttering a string of words that he was sure were the cause of the cashier's reaction. Stepping from the car, he stopped her.

"Rose, what's wrong?"

Rose looked into his face. Her anger and frustration peaked. "I can't wear red." Near the edge of collapse from the emotions that raged within, she surrendered to the comfort of his arms.

"You don't have to," he whispered. Back in the car, he wrapped his arms protectively around her.

He found the size and color she needed at another store and walked to the bathroom door with her. Rose fumbled with the bag dropping it on the floor. Dennis picked up the bag and took Rose into the restroom. Even battle-hardened soldiers need time away from the war. A time to heal, to renew or they would shut down, their system no longer able to handle the strain. Closing the door behind him Dennis removed Rose's shoes.

She felt detached, as if, she was watching Dennis dress someone else. Her mind took her back to another time and place. A time where deep blue eyes the color of the sea were filled with love and passion, a place where firm strong hands were gentle in their caressing.

As Dennis pulled the nylons up her legs, he tried to focus on the day, the funeral of his brother. He tried, and failed. His fingers trembled as they slid along the satin texture of her legs.

"Rose," he adjusted her skirt, "Rose…we can go now."

Blue passion changed to black heat as Dennis's face came into focus.

Forcing back the lethargy of despair, Rose attempted a smile that only partially registered on her face. "I look a mess," she declared. She flipped up her hair and let it fall haphazardly around her shoulders.

"Rose, you look fine." Fighting the need to crush her in his arms and ravage her lips, he brushed a lock of her hair back behind her ear. "We need to be going"*...before I kiss you...*"before Mother comes and reminds us we are running late."

"What would she say about us in the Women's toilet together." There was a hint of laughter in her voice as she pictured the scene.

"Let's just say, it would ruffle more than a few of her feathers."

She watched as a quirky smile appeared on his face.

Shalinn's agitation was evident as they returned to the car.

"It's about time," she huffed. "If you want to be late for a funeral, be late for your own."

"Shal." Bill's gruff retort ended the conversion.

A few minutes later Bill turned into the parking lot of the Hickory Road Baptist Church. The media was present to pay homage to another of America's fallen sons. Allowing the nation, for which they served and died to share in the final pages of a life given in sacrifice so far from home.

The church was built of light brown bricks and had a brown roof. Above the front door was a white steeple pointing to the sky. There was a playground next to the parking lot that had two small trees that one day would provide shade for children who played on the swings.

The funeral director met them and walked with them around the building. Entering through the back door, they were shown into a small room where they could wait.

The pastor came and sat with the family. He was a young man in his early thirties. A light brown beard covered his face.

"I wanted to have a word of prayer with you before we go up." The pastor bowed his head. "Lord, we come to you in a difficult hour. This family has lost so much, a son, a husband, and a father who will never see his child. They need Your strength. They need to feel Your hand of love upon their lives. We ask Your blessing for them in this hour in the name of Your precious Son. Amen.

The time approached, the director came and ushered the family in. Those in attendance stood out of respect for the grieving family.

She appreciated the strength and support of Dennis's arm as they walked down the aisle. Her feet seemed like lead weights that took all her effort just to place one in front of the other. The casket, placed in front of the pulpit was draped with an American flag. A picture of Mark, resplendent in his marine dress blues, stood on a stand to the side.

When they were all seated, an organ began softly playing. A man stood, sheltered from view by a wall of flowers, and began singing "In the Garden". His rich baritone voice resounded off the stained glass windows and cathedral ceiling with the promise of healing comfort and peace.

The pastor stood. "Mark Anthony Grady, born February 10, 1959. Died in the service of his country, October 23, 1983. The son of Retired Navy Commander William Dennis Grady and Shalinn Grady, he was united in marriage to Rose Ann Shawnassy in Jacksonville, North Carolina on September 8, 1983."

"He is survived by his wife and parents, a stepbrother; William Dennis Grady Junior, of Nashville, Tennessee; and other relatives and friends."

The pastor sat and the music played. Again, the voice of the soloist filled the auditorium. "Rock of Ages, cleft for me, let me hide myself in Thee…"

The pastor rose as the last of the music faded away. "Mark Anthony Grady graduated from the Nashville Central High School. He was active in sports and the youth program here at the church where he faithfully attended with his family. After high school, Mark followed a long family history of military service by enlisting in the United States Marine Corps.

"From an early age, growing up on military bases around the world, Mark was drawn to the marines. Was it the uniform, or the pride he saw in the men and women who wore that uniform? Maybe it was the great American history that revolves around the corps. From its inception the Marine Corps has been at the forefront of this great country's military might. For whatever the reason, when asked as a child what he wanted to be? Mark would puff out his chest and declare in a firm voice, 'I want to be a marine.'

"On a quiet Sunday morning October 23, a terrorist attack half way around the world, claimed Mark's life and the lives of 270 other marines, sailors and army personnel. They died in a war that has gone on since Joshua entered the Promised Land, and will continue until the time of Christ's return.

"A single cowardly act of terrorism, by those who share neither our dreams, nor our quest for peace in a troubled land, has brought this conflict home to America, to Nashville and the Grady family. In its wake, we are left with the memories of shattered dreams and broken promises.

"Rose." The pastor's voice was full of sympathy and tears filled his eyes. "Life without Mark, without his strength to support you, and his love to comfort you, will not be easy.

"At times like these, it's easy to have bitterness and hatred replace the grief and sorrow we feel as we try to answer the question- Why?

"I have a letter, from Mark, that I have been asked to read, should this day ever be reached." He wiped the tears from his eyes.

*Dear Pastor:*

*Many question why we are involved in a war that has no apparent end. Until recently, I too have had questions. I have looked into the eyes of children, the hope for tomorrow, and realized that we are their hope for an end of the bloodshed that ravages this land. The other day a hospital corpsman and I helped deliver a Palestinian baby. The woman couldn't understand us and we couldn't understand her but she knew we were there to help. As I looked into her eyes filled with the travail of childbirth, there was also a look of trust. That mantel is sometimes difficult to wear, and sometimes costly to bear. If I am called to pay that cost, to make that sacrifice, I do it not only in the service to my country but in the service to my Lord.*

*Tell my wife Rose, who I love dearly not to grieve too long, but to be strong, as I know she can and will be. Thank my parents for their love and support through all the years. Thank you Pastor most of all, for showing me faith in Christ.*

Signed; *Mark Grady, Sergeant, United States Marines*

"Rose, as you, and the family struggle in the days and weeks ahead to put this tragedy behind you and go on with your lives, know this. In the hallowed halls of heaven, Sergeant Mark Grady is standing his post. In the time honored traditions of the corps, from Montezuma to Tripoli, from the beaches of Normandy, and the hills of Iwo Jima, to the rice paddies of Vietnam, and now Lebanon, and Grenada, the battle cry to carry on was, is and shall ever be, 'Semper Fi.'"

The pastor sat and the organ softly played.

The soloist sang, "Lord, I'm Coming Home."

A quiet reverent hush fell over the building as the notes drifted up to the halls of heaven. The Marine Honor Guard acting as pallbearers rose as one. With delicate care, they bore their fallen brother down the aisle of the church.

Rose, supported by Dennis, followed on trembling legs as Mark began his final journey as a marine.

All along the three mile drive to the Military National Cemetery, men in uniform snapped to attention. Fireman, policeman, Veterans of Foreign Wars and the American Legion all joined in paying tribute and honor as the procession passed.

At the cemetery, Rose noticed the white stones in a field of green, all perfectly aligned, each looking like the others around it. Only the names chiseled in cold stone showed any distinction between the graves.

"It doesn't matter," she whispered softly.

"What doesn't matter, Rose," Dennis strained to hear.

"Whether they were rich or poor, officer or not. In here they are all the same…," her voice broke.

"Men of honor, duty, and a love for their country." Dennis finished for her.

At the gravesite, the pastor read the Twenty-third Psalm and recited the Lord's Prayer.

Rose flinched with every round fired as if waiting for the impact of the bullets. The echoes faded, the sound of a lone bugle, mournfully playing Taps, floated across the cemetery lawn. The honor guard stepped to the casket. With sharp, defined military precision, they folded the American flag.

"Mrs. Grady, on behalf of the president of the United States, the commandant of the Marine Corps and a grateful nation, I present you with this flag. I extend to you our most profound sympathy at your loss." The Lieutenant stepped back and saluted.

Rose clutched the folded flag to her breast and accepted the condolences of those that passed by. Dennis placed his arm compassionately around her shoulders.

"The ladies of the church have prepared a meal for the family," the pastor informed them. "We want you to know you have our utmost sympathy. If there is anything else we can do, please, do not hesitate to ask."

Arriving back at the church Rose didn't want to eat, she didn't want the company of virtual strangers no matter how meaningful their actions were.

Dennis filled her a plate and carried it to her. He knew she was hurting, they all were. "Please Rose, if not for yourself for the baby. Just try to eat something.

Her body was on automatic. Rose ate without tasting, without thinking. Surprised that the plate was empty she realized that she was feeling better. Not great, but definitely better. The mere act of doing something had freed her mind to begin healing. Thanking the ladies who prepared and served the food, she followed the rest of the family to the car.

# Chapter Twelve

"I think I'll rest awhile." Rose informed them upon arriving back at the house.

Setting her small clutch purse and Mark's flag on the dresser she undressed. Adjusting the water temperature Rose stepped lethargically into the shower and leaned wearily against the shower wall.

Dennis changed clothes and heard the shower still going. They had been home over half an hour. Concerned, he knocked lightly on the door. "Rose."

Receiving no response, he opened the door. Through the etched glass of the shower door, he saw her curled up on the floor. Opening the door, he turned the water off. Gently Dennis caressed her hair.

"Rose." Taking a towel, he covered her shoulders. "Rose." She looked up with reddened eyes. The sight caused his heart to break. "Come, let me help."

Picking her up, he carried her to the bed. *Damn. Here she was grief stricken with a broken heart and I am responding physically to her.*

"Rest a while." He consoled her as he turned back the covers.

"Don't go Dennis. Hold me. Please," she pleaded. "I feel so alone."

Rose crawled into his lap and wrapped her arms around him. Rocking her as gently as he would a child,

Dennis was all too aware that her firm breast was pressed against his heart. With his other arm around Rose, the weight of her other breast rested disturbingly on his hand. He fought the burning desire to cup her full weight. Her breath on the side of his neck heated his blood until his whole body felt on fire. So absorbed with the inner conflicts that were warring within, he failed to hear the door as it opened.

"Dennis!" The angry retort split the air.

Dennis jerked around and Rose reached for the sheet. All to aware, by the scandalous look on Shalinn's face, how this must look.

"How dare you?" She spat out in unmasked hostility. "The dirt hasn't evens settled on Mark's grave and already you are seducing my other son."

Shalinn advanced purposely across the floor, her breathing rapid and shallow, and her eyes livid. Rose watched the hand rise to strike, as the hand descended, it was blocked by Dennis.

"I want you out of my house." she snarled. "Do you understand? Today!" She turned and stomped out the door.

"Mother," Dennis hurried after her. "Let me explain."

"Explain! I don't need you to explain what I can see with my own two eyes."

"Mother," Dennis pleaded, "its not what you think."

"Enough! You hear me!" Shalinn whirled around. "You don't like my decision, then you can leave right along with her!"

Going back to Rose's room, he watched as she threw her few things into the suitcase.

"Call me a cab please." She threw her hairbrush at the case.

"Rose, let me talk to her after she calms down."

She chuckled, "That's the first thing I've had to laugh at today, and I don't feel much like laughing. She comes in finds me like this in your arms and you want to talk to her. Now that's funny." Rose picked up a bra and panties and slipped them on.

"The sooner you call the cab the quicker I can be gone." Putting on her blouse on she reached for a skirt. "Just go Dennis, there's nothing more to see here."

A few minutes later Rose descended the stairs with as much dignity as she could muster and set the case by the door. She found Dennis and his Father in the kitchen.

"Did you call a cab?" she addressed Dennis. When she got no response, she threw her hands in the air. "Bill, please tell Shalinn that I appreciate all that you have done, and I regret the embarrassment that I have caused"

"I'm taking you to the airport Rose," Dennis informed her.

"I'm sorry Rose," Bill apologized. "Right now Shalinn is distraught, as we all are over Mark's death. Dennis explained what happened. Unfortunately she won't listen right now, even to me."

"Maybe it is best this way," Rose reasoned. "This way we can all get back to our lives."

Dennis answered the ringing phone. "When?"

"Are you sure?" Every nerve went on alert, warning bells started going off in his head.

"Okay." His mind was racing with the different possibilities this information meant. "Listen, get out, now.

Don't call here again. Go to where we had coffee the other morning."

Rose watched as he hung up the phone. Dennis turned to his dad with a troubled look on his face.

"Change of plans. Barney and his computer are missing.

"Frank questioned a cleaning lady. He was seen about an hour ago leaving with three men, all wearing suits. When Frank last saw Barney, he had gotten into Richard's file through another access, but then run into another lock. When he came back Barney was gone along with his electronic toys."

Bill pondered the problem, picked up the phone, and started to dial and just as quickly hung up. "Pack a bag, be ready to leave when I get back."

Dennis noticed the light flashing on the side of the phone. "Didn't take long to get a tap," he commented.

"Be ready, I won't be long." His father advised as he walked out the door.

Dennis went to the cabinet and pulled out his revolver and shoulder holster.

"Is that necessary?" She noticed the grim expression on his face and her own fear began to build.

"I hope not…but I feel safer at this point having it with me, at least until this deal with Richard is over."

An hour later, Bill returned and handed Dennis a bank sack and gave Rose a kiss on the cheek. "Now go, and don't worry about mother, everything will be alright. I'll have a talk with her when she calms down."

They had gone only a few miles when he pulled into a parking lot and stopped. "What's wrong Dennis?" All this cloak and dagger was starting to scare her.

"I don't know what can of worms we opened when we started looking into Richard's background. We know the CIA is looking for him and why. I wonder who else?" His eyes never stopped moving from the area around them as he weighed his options.

"This car and any plastic cards we use can be easily traced." Starting the car, he pulled back onto the street. A short while later, he pulled into a marina.

Rose watched as he made a call, picked up the luggage, and headed for the pier.

"Don't just sit there, let's go!" he demanded.

She had no choice but to follow.

Dennis cast off the stern line from a forty-foot cabin cruiser and climbed aboard.

She looked at the stern and read the name. *Country Lady.*

Reaching down he assisted Rose onto the deck.

"Whose yacht?"

"Belongs to a client who is on tour and won't be back for a while." He stowed the ladder. "I've never used it, now seemed like a good time to take her up on her offer to do so." Dennis climbed up to the bridge. "Cast off the bow line when I signal."

Dennis started the engines and checked the gages. He gave Rose the signal and the bowline dropped away. Backing away from the pier he headed down river.

"What about the car?" She asked as she climbed to the bridge. "If they located it at the marina they will know we are on the river."

"Taken care of." Dennis maneuvered through the traffic that abounded around Nashville and was soon on open water with only the barges to contend with.

The bow spray created a fine mist in the air, and with the wind in her hair Rose felt refreshed. Exuberance bubbled in her veins like fine champagne. For the moment she forgot about bombing, pushed aside Mark's death, and the funeral she had attended only hours ago.

They sped down river until almost dark. Dennis backed into a small cove and dropped anchor. The main channel was barely visible from the boat.

Rose checked out the galley, found a fully stocked pantry of canned goods, and bottled water. Enough staples to see them through several days. The only thing they lacked was fresh meat.

The whip-o-wills were starting their nightly serenade. Somewhere on shore, an owl hooted. Rose sat looking out over the water.

"Go ahead, take a swim." Dennis encouraged. "I'll be below."

She watched his retreating back disappear down the ladder. Looking around at her surroundings, she stripped down to her underwear, and then hesitated as she looked toward the door that Dennis had gone through. Removing her bra and panties she slipped into the water.

Dennis resisted the desire to watch her. He really didn't need to see her to remember ever curve of her velvety skin. After this afternoon, she would be a permanent memory that would be impossible to forget, even if he wanted to. He felt the boat rock with her weight as she climbed aboard.

"Thanks for the towel." She entered the galley drying her hair.

Dennis watched her with building desire. Her damp skin caused her blouse to mold itself to her like a second skin. The nipples, enlarged from the contact with the chilly water showed plainly.

Rose watched his eyes darken with desire. She was standing close enough to see the pulse in his neck beating rapidly.

"I'll have supper fixed in a few minutes." Her voice sounded raspy and sultry even to her. She felt the warmth of desire pool between her legs. *This is so wrong. I shouldn't feel these things for Dennis.*

Dennis went on deck and waited. He didn't think a swim would help cool his desire. A short frustrating wait followed until Rose handed him a warmed up plate of beans and a slice of canned ham. "I brought you a beer, found a couple in the back of the fridge."

"Thanks," he took the plate. "You bunk up front; I'll take one of the beds in the galley." He took the plate, went up to the bow, and ate.

He sat in the colored glow of the running lights and looked out over the gentle ripples on the water. The boat rocked ever so slightly. Noises came from the kitchen and then directly underneath him. Rose had gone to bed. Her words in the café came back to him, "I don't wear a nightgown." *Damn you Mark.* The night sounds from the tree line floated across the water to mock him. *Damn you for dying and leaving a woman like Rose behind.* He crushed the beer can in his hand. The tears flowed down his cheeks and splattered on his shirt. *Damn you, little brother, for leaving me.*

The next morning Rose woke to a pitching bed and the vibration of the diesel engines. She warmed up last night's leftovers and carried them on deck.

"Thanks for making the coffee this morning. Hope you don't mind leftovers." She handed him the plate. "We need to stop somewhere and get a few fresh supplies."

"We'll stop somewhere up ahead," he informed her. "Take the wheel while I eat."

Rose zipped her jacket against the early morning chill.

For an hour, he kept scanning the shoreline. Seeing a small marina he pulled up to the pier. "Go up and get the supplies we need while I fuel."

"How long do you think we will be out here?" Rose inquired as she jumped to the pier.

"I have no idea." Dennis ran his hand through his wind swept hair. "Plan for a week. If we need more supplies we can stop somewhere else."

"A week." She muttered as she briskly headed for the store at the end of the pier. "This is going to be one very long week."

Dennis filled the tank and entered the store. "What's Gunny's number."

A few minutes later, he returned from making the call.

"Find out anything?"

He paid the bill and headed towards the boat. "Nothing so far." He jumped aboard and assisted Rose. "Frank has an idea where they took Barney. He hasn't seen a trace of Richard."

"Any chance of the goons who took Barney finding out anything from him?"

"Not willingly." Dennis started the engines and pulled away from the pier. "Depends on how inquisitive they are or if this is just a scare tactic." He maneuvered the yacht around some small fishing boats and continued.

"Barney was Navy Intelligence and went through SEAL training. Electronics is not only a hobby, but also his specialty. He fit perfectly into the SEAL world. Dad was his Commanding Officer in the Intelligence side. Barney got married and started a family. After seeing so many families fall apart he decided his family was more important than his career. Dad offered him a position and he jumped on it. He has never had to worry about not seeing his family again, until now." A couple of miles down river he pulled into to a wide cove that was partially hidden from view and anchored.

"Why are we stopping?"

"Because I don't know where the hell to go," he answered harshly. "Sorry, it's not your fault. I have no plan, no knowledge as to what is going on or why this is happening. All we are doing is going blindly down river and we don't know who or what we are fleeing from. Clarksville is just up ahead. I'll find a phone in the morning and call the office using an unlisted number. Maybe by then Dad will have figured out what is going on."

"In the meantime we wait," she concluded.

"We might as well enjoy ourselves," he decided. "Look like normal tourists. I'm going down and change."

A few minutes later Rose watched as he came back on deck. The trunks he was wearing were stretched like a second skin, especially in the front. Rose felt a heat flush her skin that had nothing to do with embarrassment, and everything to do with a sensual desire that captivated her thought.

Rose had found a one-piece French cut white suit. The strap between her legs didn't come close to covering her. Crimson curly hair stood out in sharp contrast to her pale skin and white suit.

She leaned her head against the bulkhead and closed her eyes. *Oh Mark, I am so confused. Why is this happening? We just laid your body to rest and already I have strong desires for your brother. I feel so disloyal to you and yet I can't fight these feelings for Dennis much longer. Please, forgive me, my love.* Going on deck, she found Dennis already in the water. She jumped in quickly before she gave herself time to change her mind.

Rose swam until the cool water had her teeth chattering. Climbing the ladder, she turned around to find Dennis right behind her.

The view he had took his breath away, and instantly affected the tightness of his trunks. The strap between her legs had folded and been pulled partially inside her.

"Your suit is transparent."

"Yours might as well be," she added.

"That's what you do to me Rose. Whenever you're close, I can't fight the attraction, even though I have tried."

Rose turned away. The passion in his voice reminded her of Mark, and the first night they made love. "I feel the same way, but it can't be. I'm Mark's widow, I'm carrying his child," her voice broke. "We buried him only yesterday and already it seems like a lifetime since he held me in his arms. This attraction will pass. It just has to."

"Why must it pass?" he placed his hands on her shoulders and gently turned her around.

"Because if it doesn't, then I will be as Richard said. 'A slut and a whore'."

"Dear Rose. Such a beast as Richard doesn't deserve a daughter as you." He drew her close and encircled her in his arms. "You could never be that. You are too pure and courageous to ever be that type of person. I know that now and Mother will too, in time."

Rose pushed away, a tear falling slowly down her face. "I look into your eyes and see the same desire that I feel inside. That is why we must both resist this. Nothing more than a few hours of pleasure can come from it. Our worlds are too far apart." She turned and went below.

Dennis knew deep down that she was probably right, but that didn't stop the desire. He damned Richard all over again for the abuse she had suffered at his hand.

That evening Rose was in pain, being outside in the afternoon sun had felt wonderful. However, her pale skin was now the color of a cooked Lobster. Even the light cotton shirt caused her to wince as she put it on.

"Here," he offered. "Let me put this on your sunburn."

Turning away from him she slowly removed the shirt. Flinching as it rubbed against her skin.

"You are going to be hurting later." He poured a generous amount of aloe burn cream in his hand.

"What do you mean later?" She mumbled as she lay face down on the bed. "It already hurts."

Rose gasped as the cream touched her fevered skin. Within moments, she felt relief from the sunburn. Only to be replaced by another burn deep within which threatened to scorch her very soul. Dennis moved to the back of her legs. She tensed when his hand slid up high on the inner thighs. A little voice from within screamed at her to stop this madness, which was spiraling out of control. Almost on their own accord, her legs spread giving him more access. The skirt she had on inched higher with each movement of his hand. When his fingers lightly touched her panties, she shuddered at the contact.

Rose sat up and twisted in his arms. Taking his face in her hands she kissed Dennis open mouthed, explosively and full of promise. His hand stroked her side and cupped her breast. Need overcame the doubts. Desire overcame the voice of reason. His mouth left hers and she cried out. The cry became of gasp of pleasure as his tongue encircled the sensitive nipple of her breast. Straddling his legs, she ground her pelvis into his, wanting and needing more.

Dennis turned and fell backward on the bed taking Rose with him. He felt her hand on the waistband of his shorts and lifted his hips to accommodate her as he tore at her clothing. She towered above him, her breast firm and beautiful. As she lowered herself onto him, he thrust upward making the union complete.

Riding with wild abandon, she matched each move, growing bolder as the sensations racking her body increased. Just as she thought she could endure no more she felt him explode deep inside her, triggering her own release. Collapsing on his chest, she found his mouth in a hot embrace. He was still nestled inside her as their bodies shook with the after shocks of their union.

His heart rate slowed. Shaken by what they had just shared he held Rose tight against his chest. In the heat of passion, her eyes had turned to molten jade, sprinkled with a sea of golden stars. A rumble sounded from deep within him.

"I suppose I have to feed you now." She teased, lightly brushing her hair across his face.

"If you don't mind," he kissed her nose. "You are such a wild passionate woman. I find myself weak. Feed me before I faint away."

Seductively she moved her hips. Feeling him harden inside her Rose sat up, driving him deeper still. The satisfying moan that escaped his lips drove her on.

Rose gently moved off of Dennis, scooted off the bed, and looked down at him. Her eyes searched his body, memorizing the scar across his chest and another just below the waist that arched from mid-thigh to where his penis lay curled in a cushion of hair.

"You have some painful memories."

"We both do Rose," he whispered. "We both do."

She leaned over and kissed him. "Let's go up on deck and eat."

The night was exceptionally warm for November as Dennis spread a blanket on the deck. Rose came through the hatch carrying a couple plates balanced in one hand and a couple sodas in the other. The lights cast moving shadows on her as she walked across the deck. He patted a cushion beside him and she sat down with her back to his chest.

"Hmmm, a light repast of healthy finger foods." Reaching around her he picked up a piece of cheese and touched her lips. The feeling that ran through him when she took the food from his fingers was like an adrenalin rush, supercharging his body.

As they fed each other their awareness grew. With each touch, each licking the flavor of food from the other's fingers their breathing deepened. Taking a cherry tomato, he dipped it in dressing and started to feed it to her when it slipped from his fingers and rolled between her breasts leaving a creamy trail behind.

Dennis shifted and laid Rose on the blanket. Starting where the trail of the tomato began, he licked the dressing from her skin.

The lower his tongue went, the tighter she gripped the blanket. Every place his lips touched burned 'til her whole body felt on fire. Her moan of pleasure and gasp of delight floated on the wind as his mouth covered hers and his tongue invaded her body. His tiny nips at her tender flesh and the healing kisses had her writhing in ecstasy. When she thought she couldn't take any more he moved up her body capturing a nipple gently with his teeth. She arched her body at the contact to her ultra sensitive breasts and felt his hard length slide inside her. Wrapping her arms around him, she held on as he slowly led the way to where they stood inside the circle of fire that had consumed and renewed lovers since the beginning of time.

In the twilight of the evening, they sat curled up in each other's arms, watching the stars and listening to the night sounds of the river. They fell asleep in each other's arms, the Indian summer night breeze gently rocked the boat and covered their naked flesh much like a lover's caress.

Before dawn, he carried a sleeping Rose below deck. Slipping on a pair of shorts, windbreaker and deck shoes, he returned topside and raised the anchor.

Rose was just coming up the ladder when he moored next to the pier of a moderately sized marina. "Morning, sleep well?" As she stretched, the material of her shirt pulled taunt across her breast and rode up her thigh.

"Best rest I've had in weeks."

"We're in port, you might want to put something on besides a T-shirt.

Rose turned and fled back down the ladder as Dennis laughed.

After a hearty breakfast at the marina café, he called the office.

When he returned to the table she noticed his gloomy face. "Nothing yet?"

"No, and nothing from the Ferret either. Neither Dad nor Gunny has heard from him. Let's go."

Rose stood beside him on the bridge as they headed down river. "Problems?" She placed her hand on his arm. There was an edge to his voice that hadn't been there earlier.

"Too many question and no answers." Dennis gave her a quick kiss. "There have been several strangers in and out of the café the last couple of days. Frank has apparently gone underground. May not hear from him for a couple of days."

"Will he be all right?" Worry over Frank edged her voice.

"Unless he gets careless, and in all the years I have known him that's one thing he isn't. He told me about his work as an instructor at the agency. 'Never teach the student all you know, save something for the unexpected' If someone is looking for him, he is enjoying the hunt. The wise old fox against a pack of puppies in their Harvard suits and patent leather shoes."

They found a cove with a sandy beach, miles from nowhere. Dennis built a fire on the beach to ward off the cool north breeze. Rose sat cuddled in his arms. The firelight danced in her hair. The picture brought back the dream he had had, and woke up to find his fingers clutching at her arms. The moon came out bathing their private cove in a soft-lit glow.

"Want to join me in a swim?" He invited as he dropped his shorts and stood naked before her. Her eyes grew sultry in the reflected light of the dancing flames. She pulled the tee shirt over her head and dropped her own shorts in the sand. He felt the desire, never far from the surface, burning within.

"Maybe the swim can wait?" He whispered.

His ridged length beckoned to her. She grew moist at the thought of him being inside her again. Rose held out a hand. "I have no problem waiting," she purred.

# Chapter Thirteen

He joined her on the sand, tasting her lips and the sweetness within. Hungry for her, his kisses left a trail down her neck to rest upon the firmness of a breast. His fingers trailed a feathery path down her side to glide across her hip and settle on the mound of soft curls between.

A deep moan of desire came from Rose as he slipped a finger inside and gently stroked the innermost petals of this delightful rose.

Unwilling to wait any longer, she pulled at his shoulder urging him to cover her. She could no more stop the moan of pleasure that escaped her lips than she could stop the sun from rising or the ocean tide from crashing on the shore. The pleasure and passion deepened as they moved in unison on the sand. She felt his warmth fill her; her own climax racked her body. Dennis rolled over taking her with him. She felt the after tremors subside and his heart rate slow. Rose kissed him.

"I think I would enjoy that swim now."

"If you have such an aversion to the CIA." She asked after their swim. "How did you and Frank get to be such good friends?"

"I met Frank in Saigon and we became good friends." Dennis opened the door to his past. "Nixon had already begun pulling regular troops out when I was assigned to the South Vietnamese Army. At the time congress was pulling the troops out, they were dumping large amounts money and equipment into the South Vietnamese Army. They were equipped and trained better than the enemy but they had lost the weight of the American forces and the will to fight. When North Vietnam attacked in January 1975 they folded. When that happened, Frank and I were on our own as were others who weren't there, officially.

"Before we got back to the world, we were like brothers. Neither of us trusted the Vietnamese so we had to trust each other and watch each other's back.

"We hid for several days as the city erupted in violence. Many South Vietnamese who had worked for and with the Americans were slain. In the middle of the night when it was raining so hard that you couldn't distinguish between friend and foe, we made our way onto the base and stole a boat. By the time we were noticed, we had disappeared in a wall of rain and darkness.

"I gave him Dad's number and basically told him, 'any time you get tired of the Agency, you've got a job waiting.' About two years later, he showed up on the doorstep. He has been with us ever since."

Rose lost track of the hours and days. Her burn faded and her skin turned a deep copper. Tan lines were absent from her golden flesh. She watched Dennis as he fished in the shallow waters of the cove. They swam, made love on the beach, and cooked over the open fire. Time stood still in their little haven of paradise. She dreamed it would last forever.

Reality came back one morning when Dennis announced. "I need to check in again with the office to see if there is any news."

They pulled out of the cove toward the river's channel, she looked back and said goodbye to her little dream world.

Dennis pulled into the marina they had been to last. Tying off the bowline, he jumped to the pier. "Be right back."

A few minutes later Dennis returned and climbed aboard. "Let go the bow line, Rose." He instructed as he started the engines.

Pointing the bow upriver, he opened the throttle. "Dad said they turned Barney loose two days ago." He shouted over the noise of the diesels. "About the time Frank got ready to nab Richard, he spotted the agency boys and hid. Frank hasn't located him again."

The next day, with both taking turns at the wheel Dennis pulled into the Nashville Marina. His car was waiting in the parking lot.

"Dennis, I need to get back to Jacksonville and the café," she announced. "I've been gone too long now."

Stunned, with what they had shared on the river, that she could just up and casually leave he asked. "What about us?"

"My dear sweet Dennis," she whispered. "I thought you realized, there is no *us*. What we shared, I will always treasure. There will never be another to hold a place in my heart the way you do. This is your home and you have a business to run, as I do. Gunny is a good cook but he has never handled the books with any propriety. I must go. I will miss you as I would life itself." Rose lied to herself in fear that he might see her true feeling for him and not let her go.

"You're going, just like that?" His words took on the bite of bitterness and unbelief. "You used me."

Rose smiled sadly and thought of all the days and nights they had laid in each other's arms. "If that be true Dennis, at least be honest. We used each other." She walked over to a pay phone and dialed a cab.

A few minutes later, the cab arrived. She loaded her luggage and stood in front of Dennis. "Tell Bill and Shalinn I'll keep in touch. Let them know how their grandchild is doing." She stood on tiptoe to give him a kiss. Dennis backed up from her. "Please don't hate me. This is something I have to do."

Only as the cab pulled away from the marina did she allow the tears to come.

* * * * *

Unobserved among the end-of-the-day last-minute customers, Richard walked into the North Carolina Bank and Trust just before closing. Slipping into the bathroom he quickly removed a ceiling panel and pulled himself through the opening, as he dropped the panel back in place, the door opened. Waiting was the easy part. For years, he had been waiting, planning. Now he was reduced to this, hiding in a bank ceiling waiting for it to close.

Checking his watch, he removed the panel and climbed down. All Richard had to do now was to wait until the supervisor showed up. First thing in the morning when she opened the vault, he would help himself. "This wouldn't have been necessary if that bitch hadn't left Florida," he whispered angrily to the four walls.

When darkness fell, he left the confining little room. Having his fill of little rooms in the last three and a half years, he was glad to be moving. All that time and no trial, confined in a separate facility than the regular prisoners he saw no lawyers, made no phone calls, just his jailer, a cell and small exercise yard. All the CIA said they wanted was the list. The damn list, which was now lost, along with the two hundred grand promised for it. Knowing now, what he didn't know then, he would have told them where it was. Just his damn bad luck running true to form.

Disabling the cameras and the security system, he sat down to wait out the night.

The next morning, Richard watched from the partially open bathroom door as the supervisor and head teller entered the bank. The supervisor set her handbag on the desk, stepped over to the vault door, and released the lock. When they stepped inside, Richard moved to the door, slipped a stocking cap over his face, and calmly entered.

"Ladies, kindly step away from the safe and turn around." The shock on their faces was joy. He hadn't seen that much fear on a woman's face in four years. "Lie down on the floor and place your hands behind your back," he ordered. "Now! Get down there before I have to hurt you!"

Both women dropped to the floor and Richard, using the bank's duct tape, which he had found during the night, taped their hands and feet. For good measure, and the pain it would inflict when removed, he wrapped the tape completely around their heads. Turning to the safe, he smiled. "Like taking candy from a baby." Picking up a large bank sack, he started filling it with cash, tens, twenties, fifties, and another bag for the hundreds. "Thank you, ladies," he smirked. "Pleasure doing business with you."

Going out the back door, he calmly made his way down the alley. Stopping behind a dumpster Richard quickly changed into a pair of baggie sweats and tennis shoes. Sticking the moneybags into the empty gym bag, he jogged down the street. A mile down the road he turned into another alley and slipped into a vacant house. He smiled as the sound of sirens filled the air. Taking off the latex gloves, he stashed the sacks of money with those he had taken previously. One more bank job and there would be enough to leave, but not before he paid the little bitch another visit. He had a score to settle with her and her interfering boyfriend.

* * * * *

Rose settled into her new role at Gunny's Café, thankfully she found little time for dwelling on the past. Her waistline seemed to be expanding daily. She could feel the tiny movement as the baby kicked and turned. There was nothing she could do about the broken stone in her chest that had once been her heart. The die had been cast. She had to make the best of it, for herself and the baby.

A cold blast of air raced across the café to announce another customer had opened the door. Rose looked up at the person and recognized Linda's smile peering out of the fur-lined hood. The bundle in her arms could only be Jason Jr.

"Linda!" Rose stepped around the counter and gave her a hug. "What brings you down to the strip? Oh! Let me have him."

Rose reached out, lifted the baby from Linda's arms, and sat him on her own expanding stomach. "You are getting so big. Yes you are." She kissed Jason's little nose. "One of these days my baby will be here and the two of you can grow up together, attend the same school." Inhaling the fresh baby fragrance, Rose felt a fresh wave of movement of her child.

"I think my little one wants to come out and play with you. What do you think?" Jason Jr. cooed and smiled as Rose gently rocked him in her arms.

"That's why I'm here Rose. I came to say goodbye."

"You're leaving early for the Christmas holidays? That will give you more time with your family. I hope you have a safe trip there and back."

"Rose, you don't understand, I'm not coming back. I just couldn't tell you sooner. Sorry."

Rose held the baby in one arm, and Linda with the other. "Isn't this a little sudden? You're sure this is for the best."

"Ever since I went home at Thanksgiving I have been trying to decide. I have a lot of friends here, but all my family lives in Iowa. I finally made my decision. I sold our house, Jason's motorcycle and anything else I won't need."

"I'm going to miss the two of you. Shall we sit? Have you eaten?" Rose rambled.

"I am going to miss you too Rose. I can't stay long, maybe just a cup of hot chocolate if you have any. The movers are coming tomorrow and I still have a ton of things to do."

Little Jason started to fidget and Linda reached for him.

Rose watched as she opened her coat and unfastened a couple of buttons. Jason quieted and began sucking when placed against her breast.

"I'll bring the chocolate." They had become friends through shared sorrow. Now she was loosing her too. *Just like I lost Dennis.*

Rose sat down and Linda shifted Jason to a more comfortable position.

"Heard anything from Dennis?" Linda saw the hurt, which Rose tried to hide, with the sudden shift of her eyes away from her.

"No, why should I? Just as you made your decision about leaving, I made mine about Dennis. You've burnt your bridges behind you just as I have. We have to live with those decisions Linda."

The tightening of the smile and the slight drop of the shoulders told Linda more than what Rose was saying. She smiled. If only her mind would listen to her heart.

"Rose there is always a new bridge to cross, don't burn all of them. I have to go, I just wanted to see you before I left. I hope you and the baby will be fine." She stood and gave Rose a hug. "Think about what I said."

She was thinking, every night when she went to bed, alone. She looked at Gunny working in the kitchen alongside the new cook. He wasn't getting any younger and he needed her. The sadness in his eyes whenever she caught him watching her disturbed her. She placed her hand over her expanding waist. This was the right thing; she had gone over it in her mind. It was the only thing she could do.

* * * * *

Back in Nashville, the late December weather matched Shalinn's feelings. She had had it with the cold, the snow, and Dennis's surly nature. She had come to accept the idea of Rose and Dennis being together. The way Dennis was acting, said more than what he wasn't saying. She didn't want to interfere, but something had to be done.

"If you can't be more civil around here then find your own place to live. I am tired of you snapping at everyone and everything and I am not going to put up with your short-tempered cantankerous attitude. It's not only me, several of our friends have commented on it too. I think it is absolutely disgusting, you're moping around here lusting after your brother's wife."

"That's it!" he boiled. "I have had all this I am going to take. I am going, something I should have done when I came back from the service. And for you information I do care about Rose, very much."

"That's the biggest lie you have ever told." Shalinn stood in the middle of the kitchen floor with her hands on her hips. "If that were the truth, you wouldn't still be here. You would've hauled your backside out of here a long time ago and convinced her you care. You haven't even called to see how she was doing, have you? If she turned you out on your ear, I wouldn't blame her. You said you were going, so go. Just make sure you know which direction you're heading."

Dennis threw clothes into a suitcase and then filled another. At twenty-nine, it was past time to be on his own. Finished packing, he loaded his car and left.

Bill and Shalinn watched as he drove away.

"That wasn't so difficult," she smiled.

"Think he will go after her?" Bill wondered out loud.

"If he cares about her the way I think he does. Just as soon as he admits it to himself, he will burn up the road heading east."

Squinting into the glare of the setting sun, Dennis pulled into a motel. A restaurant just across the street caught his attention, 'The River Wharf.' The name brought back memories of another Wharf almost two months back. A lot had happened since then. No matter how hard he tried not to, he still thought of her every day. Maybe his mother was right. Seeing Rose might get her out of his system for good.

Opening the door to his room, he switched on the television.

"Elsewhere around the nation, the police of Jacksonville, North Carolina have received their first break in a series of near perfect bank robberies, which have plagued the city for the last two months. The suspect, caught on tape as he robbed a credit union and shot a guard is believed to be the man responsible for the recent increase in the number of robberies. The police are asking the public's assistance in solving these crimes. If you know this man or his whereabouts, you are requested to call the Jacksonville Police immediately. This man is considered armed and extremely dangerous."

Dennis threw his suitcases back in the car and within minutes was headed east. It was only a matter of time before Gunny's Café would be visited by Jacksonville's latest most wanted criminal. Richard Shawnassy.

Ignoring speed limit signs he hurled towards the coast. The morning sun rising out of the Atlantic found him pulling into Gunny's parking lot. He pulled around back and parked next to Rose's Firebird.

"Morning." Gunny spoke without looking up. "Didn't figure it would take you this long to show up."

"You see the news?" Dennis closed the door.

"Yup." Gunny filled another bowl with eggs. "Figured it wouldn't be long before he paid me a visit. Surprised it's taken him this long to show up. You call the police?"

"Nope." Dennis picked up a piece of bacon and chewed thoughtfully.

Gunny looked up and smiled. "Me neither."

"Couple of questions I want to ask before I get the police involved," Dennis added.

"You can ask your questions." Gunny's voice turned hard as he took another slab of bacon and took the meat clever savagely to it. "I just want a little satisfaction for him busting up my girl's place."

"How is she?"

Gunny gave him a cross look.

"You could have called at least once to find out," he lashed out angrily. "On top of being pregnant, Rose has been like an old she-bear woke from a winter's nap. She has all of us walking around on eggshells lately." He cracked two more eggs and then crushed the shells.

Dennis quietly climbed the stairs. The door was open as usual, he heard the shower going, and he sat down to wait.

Rose turned off the shower and wrapped her head in a towel.

"Don't you ever knock?" she roared.

"Don't you ever wear clothes?" he countered.

"Not in my own damn house if I don't want to," she laughed. *She hadn't felt this lighthearted since her return.* "I think we already had this conversation" *If you want him, don't just stand there girl. Do something.* "What brings you around here after all this time?" *That's right, throw yourself at him like the cheap little whore that you are.*

"Richard," he hesitated. "You." Silently, he added from his heart, *us*.

"What about Richard?"

"Seems he has been very busy around town, the police are circulating his picture," he stated. "Figure it's just a matter of time before he shows up here."

"He's back in town?" She felt the fear return.

"If he ever left." he timidly approached where she stood.

"I suppose you think you can just waltz right back here and take up where we left off on the boat. Then when Richard is no longer a threat, prance off to Nashville again." She went back to the bedroom. "Sorry to disappoint you Dennis. You don't get what you see this time."

When Rose finished dressing, she felt a sense of disappointment at Dennis being gone. When she entered the Café, he was sitting at the counter. Gunny was lounging with his elbows on the counter, laughing at something Dennis said.

"Gunny, we won't be serving anyone breakfast on time if its not cooked," she admonished.

"See!" Gunny grumbled under his breath. "Cross as an old she-bear."

Rose checked the table and supplies for the morning. She watched Dennis out of the corner of her eye. He looked dead on his feet. Her heart took pity on him. Had he driven all night, concerned for her safety?

"Go up and get some rest before you fall asleep and drown in your coffee."

"Thanks." he tossed a bill on the table.

"Your money is no good here Dennis."

He gave a casual shrug of the shoulders and left the bill on the table. Going through the private entrance, he climbed the stairs up to her apartment.

Throughout the morning, she found herself thinking about Dennis. "By now, he is asleep on the couch, or would he have bypassed the couch for her bed." That thought brought back scenes of hot passionate days and nights on the river.

"Morning Rose." A now familiar voice spoke softly.

"Damn it Frank," she whispered. "I wish you would quit sneaking up on me like that."

"Sorry," he chuckled. "Old habits are hard to break."

"Dennis is back, got in this morning." She poured a cup and sat it on the counter.

"I saw his car around back."

"He said something about Richard, the police, and his picture on the television." She dumped the grounds and made a fresh pot of coffee.

"Did he tell you why?"

"No," she felt a forbidding chill. "Why should he?"

"Richard robbed a bank and shot a guard."

The chill became an icy hand of fear, which wrapped itself around her heart. Suppose Dennis was hurt…or worse, trying to protect her. She wasn't sure she could live with that.

"Don't worry about Dennis." Frank spoke as if reading her mind. "He can take care of himself. If it came to a pinch I can't think of anyone else I would rather have watching my back than him."

"Interesting you should say that," she mused. "I had the impression that was the way he felt about you."

"Well, I'll be going. Thanks for the coffee."

There were only a couple of customers in the café when Rose decided to take a break. An older man wearing a suit approached the counter.

"Rose Grady," he addressed her. "May I speak with you a moment? In private."

"Who are you?" she demanded.

He opened his billfold to pay for his meal.

Rose read his identification. "Agent Mitchell, FBI"

"Relax Rose." His voice smooth and practiced. "We are looking for you father."

"Who isn't," she laughed. "The police are looking for him, the CIA and now, the FBI. Before this is all over, it's going to be a zoo of who is watching whom. Tell me, are you the guys who took Barney Baker for almost a week."

"We talked to him for a while," he admitted.

"How much information did you get out of him?"

"Barney?" The suggestion made him chuckle. "He's as tight as the file he tried to get into. He almost succeeded too. We had a call from the CIA who had a visit from Frank and we called Bill Grady in Nashville. Bill is as secretive as ever," explained Mitchell.

"Come back at three, Dennis will be up by then." Rose started to walk away.

"I would rather talk privately with you," he told her.

"I'll tell you the same thing I told Agent Rodgers of the CIA. It's with Dennis, or not at all." She held his gaze and didn't back down.

"Three it is." Agent Mitchell tapped his fingers to his forehead and left.

# Chapter Fourteen

At two-thirty, Rose went up the stairs. The couch was empty and as she entered the bedroom, Dennis spoke.

"Couldn't stay away?"

"Thought you were sleeping." He still hadn't opened his eyes giving her ample opportunity to admire his naked flesh. She watched him, the part of his body that had given her so much pleasure began to stiffen and grow in size. Desire flared within her, causing her to become moist. With effort, she forced her mind back to the reason she had come up stairs.

"Agent Mitchell came by this morning." When that didn't get a response, she added. "From the FBI." He sat up in bed as if jolted by a cattle prod.

"You're just now telling me this?" he fumed. "Why didn't you tell me sooner?"

"He wants to talk. I told him to be back at three." A seductive smile played at the corners of his mouth.

"You want to make him wait awhile?" he asked. He had something pleasurable on his mind, which would cause them both to be late. If they were able to show at all.

"No!" She turned to leave the room. *Liar,* her body accused. "Get dressed, Mitchell will be here in a few minutes."

She forced her legs to carry her back down the stairs to the café.

A few minutes later Dennis followed and picked a table in the back. Rose joined him and they waited. She nervously drummed her fingers on the table. Rearranged the napkins and moved the salt and pepper shakers several times before Dennis took them out of her reach.

"Would you relax," he hissed.

At three o'clock, Agent Mitchell arrived and joined them at the back table.

"You said you wanted to talk," Rose reminded.

Mitchell looked from one to the other. "We feel that Richard may show up here soon."

"Gee, that's funny." Dennis said straight-faced. "You and the CIA for once agree on something. Only they were here sometime back."

"I have work to do before the evening rush hour," she told Mitchell. "You wanted to talk, I'm here."

"Rose." Dennis was glaring at the Agent. "Please correct me where I'm wrong," he invited. "The FBI is here because they can't find Richard, and they want our help, the same with the CIA only for a different reason. Actually between your agents and the CIA agents with their bungling and bumping into one other in their attempt to get Richard they were spotted. Once warned, Richard went to ground."

"Will you help us?" Agent Mitchell asked.

"If he shows up here we will ask him to stick around so we can call," Dennis stated sarcastically.

"He has already shot one guard. Don't do anything foolish like trying to capture him yourself. I know your reputation; I've read your military file. Don't play the hero on this one," Mitchell warned.

After Mitchell left, Rose went about making sure everything was set for the evening meal. Dennis had taken up residence in the back corner of the café. A newspaper spread out before him. She felt a degree of security knowing that he was here, while at the same time irritated that he was. Satisfied that everything was ready Rose went to the office to do her daily bookwork.

Every customer that came in got a quick going over. Apparently engrossed in the paper no one paid attention to the customer in the back booth, which was the way he wanted it. Unseen, yet able to see everything. Part of his mind drifted back to his twenty-first birthday, to an operation where blending in and waiting was the name of the game.

*It had been raining, as usual in the rain swept jungles of Vietnam. Only he was no longer in Vietnam, an hour before he had crossed the border into Laos. There was a base of North Vietnamese Regulars somewhere in the area. Rumor had it they had been reinforced by a unit of the Chinese Army. His job was to verify that rumor. Moving slow and cautiously through the hills, he had spotted several machine gun nests. This side of the border the enemy was lax. Often he had smelled their cooking fires and heard their excited chatter long before they were seen. Engaging the enemy here meant certain death. Being detected had the same outcome. In this place, death was less an evil than capture.*

*Observing a careless sentry, he had sat down to watch and wait. He smelled food cooking but couldn't detect where it was coming from. Hearing faint voices close by he froze. Shifting his eyes, he spotted a small hollow bamboo tube sticking out of the ground. Putting his ear to the tube, the voices were clear. He had found the camp, directly beneath him. Hiding in the remote jungle for five days had netted him a wealth of information. The rumor was confirmed. He had a picture of a high-ranking Chinese Officer.*

Rose came out of the kitchen and looked over the dining area. Most of the tables were full. Marching over to Dennis, she leaned over and whispered. "Look, this is a business. You are taking up a seat that could, if you weren't sitting in it, be used by paying customers. Now I appreciate what you are trying to do but you are starting to wear your welcome thin."

"I think I'll have a chicken fried steak sandwich and another cup of coffee."

His coy smile irritated her. "You misunderstood," she clarified. "I want you gone, out-of-here, as in leave. Please."

"I understood perfectly." He smiled without looking up. "You said paying customers. I just ordered, which makes me a customer. Whether or not you decide to take my money, that's your business."

Rose bristled. "You're impossible. Absolutely impossible."

"I'll have an order of fries too."

Rose stormed off muttering under her breath while his soft laughter followed like a gentle breeze.

* * * * *

Rose prepared for bed, acutely aware of Dennis in the next apartment. Ignoring his presence was impossible. When he had followed her upstairs and checked out her place before he let her go in, she had silently yelled at him to give her some space. Now that he had, she wished he hadn't. She couldn't weaken now. In a few days at the most, he would be gone again.

Dennis kept to the shadows, watching, waiting for that change in blackness that signaled movement. On this night, the shadows remained still. No figures lurked in the darkened alleys. At five-thirty, he went down to the kitchen where Gunny was mixing the dough for biscuits.

"Quiet night." Gunny added more flour.

"Too quiet," he complained. "I wish this was over."

"Me too," agreed Gunny. "So, what's your plan? Or do you have one?"

"Try to be one jump ahead of Richard when he does make a move." Dennis leaned heavily against a table. "Other than that, no. Just watch and wait. Hopefully Frank will be able to stop him before he gets here."

"You still think he's coming?" Gunny looked up at Dennis.

"Yeah. I do."

"Me too." Gunny went back to kneading the dough.

"Morning Gunny," Rose called out cheerfully. "Dennis."

He noticed the change in her voice as she spoke to him. "Morning Rose. I trust you slept well."

"You planning on taking up residence in the café all day?" she protested.

"No, I plan on going up and going to bed," he replied. "Any objections?"

"Just stay out of my hair." She turned and went back to the counter. "Keep busy," Rose told herself. The thought of him sleeping in her bed again was taking its toll on her emotions.

Dennis woke around two o'clock with a strange sensation. Unable to go back to sleep he showered and went downstairs.

Rose looked up and gave him a stern warning. The angry pucker of her lips and furious shake of the head had him retreating to the kitchen. Pete was frying burgers and gave him a wave. Picking up a fresh roll, he liberally applied butter.

Pacing back and forth in the kitchen, he felt like a caged animal. There was a nervous tension in the air, which was almost tangible. Going out the back door, he started his car and pulled out of the alley.

The agencies' promise to pull the surveillance back was a joke. He was disgusted with their involvement. One measly block was all they pulled back. One lousy damn block, they were as visible as a peacock in full strut.

The movement of a man wearing a jacket and carrying a gym bag caught his attention. Something in his movement gave Dennis a tightening of the gut and a burst of adrenalin. He took another look in the rear view mirror, the man ducked into a store.

Two blocks from the café, in broad daylight. Richard was either getting desperate or enjoyed playing a dangerous game. Parking the car at the end of the block, he watched the store entrance. Half an hour later, he knew Richard had given him the slip.

Pulling into the alley, he saw Frank picking the lock to the café. Jumping out of the car, Dennis sprinted to Frank's side.

"He spotted you," Frank whispered.

Dennis peeked through the window. Pete was lying on the floor with blood oozing from his scalp. "Yeah, I know."

The lock turned and Frank slipped inside.

Dennis unlocked the door leading to the apartment. He entered the stairway and tripped the silent alarm. Reaching the top of the stairs, he quickly checked the rooms. His heart was pounding as he descended the front stairs to the café entrance.

Dennis was going in blind. He had no idea how many customers were in there, where Richard and Rose were in relation to the door. His only hope was to distract Richard long enough for Frank to act.

Dennis eased the door open a crack.

"Come join the party Dennis." Richard called out. "I've been waiting for you. You're good; I walked right past those agency clowns. They couldn't find their butt with both hands. How long did you wait at the corner? Man I would have loved to see your face when you realized I was gone."

Richard's smile was pure evil from the sickness that had spread hate throughout his soul. Using Rose as a human shield in front of him with a Glock nine millimeter held to her head, made it impossible to try for a clean shot. Dennis tasted the bile of fear in his throat. Rose's life hung in the balance of a deranged madman's mind and yet, she stood calmly, showing no fear.

Dennis watched as the pistol moved away from Rose's head toward his own. In a flash, she twisted toward the arm holding the pistol, shoving the weapon away from him. At the same time, she jabbed Richard as hard as she could with her elbow, and dropped to the floor.

He pulled his revolver and fired.

Answering shots came from the kitchen service window. Richard spun at the impact of the four almost simultaneous shots, falling partially on top of Rose.

Gunny came running in, seeing Rose covered with blood he dropped down beside her. "Rose darling, speak to me girl. I can't lose you too."

"I'm not hurt, Gunny," she managed. "It's Richard's blood, not mine."

Frank checked Richard for a pulse, shook his head, and rolled him off Rose. I'll call an ambulance for Pete, I don't think it's serious but he needs checked out. He was starting to come to when everything broke loose."

Dennis holstered his weapon and reached down to help her up off the floor.

Frank picked up a duffel bag from behind the counter. Carrying it over to a table, he opened it. "Dennis, you might want to take a look at this."

He walked over and let out a sigh, which turned into a laugh. "How much do you think?"

"Enough for a twenty-five thousand dollar reward for its return," Frank reasoned. "They upped the reward this morning after the guard died.

The police arrived and sealed off the area. Dennis and Frank went outside and explained what had happened while those in the café were being interviewed and having their statements taken.

There was a question about using firearms and having permits. Agent Rodgers walked up to the Officer in Charge and after a few minutes conversation he left. Nothing else was said about permits or licenses.

Agent Mitchell arrived and hurriedly walked across the parking lot. "You just had to go and do it, didn't you Grady. I told you not to play the hero, but no! You risked everyone's life in there because you had to play the big shot. Now we may never find the half-million dollars he stole because you just had to shoot him. I aught to have you arrested for interfering with an official Bureau investigation."

The Police Lieutenant standing by his car observed the conversation and shook his head at the jackass who was masquerading as a Federal Law Officer. Picking up the bag, he walked over to Dennis.

"Mr. Grady." He said with tongue in cheek. "I think you might want to handle this." The Lieutenant handed him the bag, with a grin and a wink, he backed away to watch the Agent's face.

"Handle what," Mitchell blustered. "I think you have done all the handling and bungling of this that you are going to."

"Then you wouldn't be interested in this." Dennis asked with barely suppressed laughter.

"What the hell would I want with a duffel bag full of smelly clothes?"

"How about a duffel bag with a half-million dollars, would you be interested in it then?" Dennis poked him in the chest.

Mitchell backed up trying to find words as a look of shock spread across his face. Dennis followed keeping his finger on his chest. "May I suggest something, before you start spouting off about things you know absolutely nothing about, you should ask the Officer in Charge what went down at the scene." He backed the Agent up against a patrol car. "For your information Richard walked right past your agents on the street and they never saw him. He was also pointing a weapon at Rose's head. Here's your money." He forcefully shoved the bag where his finger had been jabbing. Dennis turned and walked back to the café.

The ambulance took Pete to the hospital; the coroner arrived to officially declare what everyone already knew. Richard had died from four gunshot wounds to the chest.

Rose sat in a booth; the man she had grown up knowing as her father was dead and all she felt was relief that Dennis hadn't been shot. All she could think about was the gun being pointed at Dennis. Folding her arms on the table, she lowered her head and started to shake. A comforting arm encircled her shoulders and pulled her against a solid chest.

"I was so scarred you were going to be hurt." She whispered against his shirt.

"You...scared." He kissed the top of her head. "I don't believe a word of it. I watched you, the way you remained calm. I couldn't have done better myself. Your dad would be proud of you."

Dennis realized in the instant he'd spotted the weapon at Rose's head that he loved her. Never had he known fear so real as when, he realized her life could be taken from him at any second. He didn't want a statement of love from her out of a sense of debt or gratitude. It had to be given freely, just as she had given herself to him on the boat.

Richard's body was removed and the police left, leaving the reporters who had gathered free access.

Gunny gave them a statement. "No comment." Locked the door and proceeded to scrub the blood off the floor

Dennis took Rose upstairs and removed her blood-splattered clothing.

"I can finish by myself Dennis. Thank you for being here." Pausing, she forced out the words that would plunge her into a life of loneliness. "You can go home now. You've done all you can do here." Rose went into the bathroom, closing the door behind her.

Dennis looked at the thin panel of wood that separated them. *You can run dear Rose, but you can't hide. I'm not giving up.*

Not knowing what else to do for the moment, he left. Checking into a motel, he placed a call to Bill. Tomorrow would be soon enough to begin.

The next morning a delivery truck pulled up to Gunny's Café. The driver carried in a long box.

"Are you, Rose Grady?" He handed her the box and left.

She recognized the box as coming from the most prestigious flower shop in the city. Inside she found eleven perfectly shaped roses and a gold embossed card. "Now the dozen is complete." The card was unsigned.

Rose didn't need a signature. In her heart, she knew who sent the roses. She fought the longing pull of her heart. Having made her decision in sending him away now came the hardest part, living with that decision. Knowing that the love they could have shared would never be. If her decision had been so right, why did it feel so wrong?

* * * * *

The fragrance of the roses filled the café. She found herself looking at them throughout the day. They were beautiful flowers and they were hers, but looking at the flowers reminded her of Dennis. Thinking about Dennis reminded her of so many things they had shared, grief, sorrow, comfort, desire, passion, laughter, and danger.

"I swear girl," Debbie quipped. "You act like you've never seen roses before. Or is it that you wish you had him and his roses?"

"No," she shook her head. "That wouldn't work, not permanently. Don't get me wrong; I'll always remember the week we spent on the river. Let's face it Deb, he's big city, rubbing shoulders with the top stars across the nation. Open access to their parties and nightlife. Use of their yachts at a moments notice. I'm just a pregnant, part owner of a small time café, and that's only because of Gunny's big heart."

"You know what Rose," Debbie said thoughtfully. "You keep telling yourself that long enough and one of these days that's all you will ever be, a single parent working your life away at a greasy spoon with no one to come home to. Think about it." She cocked her head and raised her eyes, turned and went back to the customers.

Pete, wearing a bandage on his head stepped out of the kitchen. Watching Rose for several minutes, he shook his head.

"What's eating you?"

Rose gave him a 'Don't you have something better to do look'. "I was just thinking," he stroked his chin. "Maybe you should have been the one to get hit over the head. It might have knocked some sense into you." Pete turned, and went back to the kitchen.

Rose slumped on the counter.

Debbie walked by and patted her on the back.

"Cheer up Rose, at least you have those beautiful flowers. Don't think they will keep you warm at night…but they smell nice."

The next morning mail brought a letter for Rose. It was postmarked in Virginia with no return address. Opening the envelope, she stared at it unbelieving.

*Dear Rose:*

*Please read this before you throw it away.*

*I have made a lot of mistakes in my life. None for which I'm more sorry for than abandoning you and your mother. I have lived with this regret for so long. My wife and I married out of convenience. By the time I met your mother, my wife was ill, slowly dieing of cancer, which took years to finally take its toll. Although there was little love between us, I couldn't abandon her to suffer alone.*

*Rose, my wife couldn't have children. Because of her illness, we couldn't adopt. You are the only child I have, the only family.*

*I know, I can never replace the kind and loving father you never knew as a child. It's probably to late to be a father to you, but I would like to be a friend.*

*I am proud of the way you turned out, your courage and loyalty. In trial and hardship, you have been tested and just like tempered steel you have been made strong. Even if you can never find it in you heart to forgive me and call me your Father, I am honored and proud to call you my daughter.*

*Thomas Rodgers*

# Chapter Fifteen

Reading the letter a second time, Rose felt the bitterness and anger that she had held in place for so long begin to slip away. A man she had never known while growing up was proud to call her his daughter, even without her forgiveness.

How could she not respond? Her heart cried out for the love she had never known from a father. She wiped at a lone tear, which slowly rolled down her cheek. Picking up the phone, she dialed information.

A few minutes later in Arlington, Virginia, a phone was ringing.

"Is Agent Thomas Rodgers there?"

"May I leave a message for him?"

"Tell Thomas that his daughter called."

"Yes, I said *daughter.*"

"No! I'm not mistaken. *I'm his daughter.*"

"Listen lady, I really don't care how many years you've known him. Just give him the message that his daughter called and that he is forgiven. He will understand."

"Thank you." She looked at the phone as if trying to see the other person. "Moron." She mumbled as she hung up the phone.

The roses faded, and Rose reluctantly threw them out. She would be glad when the baby was born. Imagine, crying over faded roses in a trashcan.

That morning, as Hank got ready to leave he snapped his finger and turned around. "Ah Rose I almost forgot. I have a package for you." He dug around in the bottom of his mailbag and pulled out a small package. "I need you to sign for it."

The return address was of a Nashville jeweler known for his special design craftsmanship and for providing the biggest stars with their evening accessories. Opening the box she gasped, inside was a pair of gold earrings shaped like miniature roses. The leaves were of jade and the flower was an intricately sculptured ruby.

"Ahh Rose! They are a workmanship of beauty."

"Yes they are," she beamed. "Thank you."

Gunny, watching from the kitchen saw the flair of amazement in Rose's face and the corresponding look on the mailman. Approaching from behind, he looked over her shoulder. The beauty of the earrings astounded him.

"Those are quite exquisite dear. You can't ignore those and stick them on a shelf. You need to thank him personally."

"I'll call right now." Picking up the phone, she dialed the Nashville number.

"Hello Bill, is Dennis there?"

"Do you know when he will be back?"

"No, I just wanted to thank him for a present he sent. Tell him I called when you hear from him."

"I'm doing fine thank you. The Doctor says everything is on schedule and the baby has a strong heartbeat. I know he has a set of strong legs or else he is going to be a fighter. Now I know what a punching bag feels like," she laughed.

"Give my regards to Shalinn."

"Bye!"

"Dennis is out of town on business, and Bill doesn't know when he will be back," she explained.

"Give the jeweler a call," Gunny suggested. "Maybe he can help?"

Rose found the number from information and dialed.

"Hello, I'm Rose Grady."

"Yes, I did. That's why I called."

"Oh, no Sir! They are lovely. I was wondering about the person who ordered them."

"Oh, I see. Thank you for your time."

"Dennis came in two weeks ago and ordered the earrings and left instructions to mail them here when they were completed." She sat dejectedly on the counter stool.

"Rose," he reminded her, "you sent him away."

Gunny's words echoed the thoughts of her accusing heart.

"It was for the best Gunny." She shut out the remembrances of tender kisses and the magical touch of his fingers.

She slipped the earrings on. "How do they look?"

"Rose. They are even more beautiful than before. I must be going, still have more mail to deliver." Hank gave a wave and was gone.

* * * * *

Dennis paced the floor of his new, Jacksonville office. Barney was out installing another security system and had an estimate to do later in the day. Looking at his watch, he noticed it was time for his interview with a prospective secretary. The last interview was with a young girl who chewed gum like a cow. She had shown up in blue jeans and a tie-dyed tee shirt. He was getting desperate for someone who could run the office while he was out.

The door opened and a woman in her early thirties walked in. This was a definite improvement over the last one. She was an attractive blonde with eyes the color of the sea. The smile she displayed was bright and cheerful. No blue jeans and no bubble gum. She already had one foot in the door.

"Hi." She reached out her hand. "I'm Maria DuBre. The employment agency sent me over. They said you were in need of a secretary with office experience."

"Please, have a seat." Dennis indicated a chair. "The information I have states that you're from Romania. You speak excellent English."

"Thank you. In Romania, they teach foreign language at an early age. I also speak French, some German, and Russian. My husband, Nicoli, and I recently escaped from Romania along with our seven-year-old daughter. He is a Doctor, but they won't accept his Romanian schooling. With him going back to school its imperative that I go back to work."

"Mrs. DuBre, the last person the agency sent over didn't have enough experience to bag groceries. What experience do you have?"

"I worked for eight years for a state-run security office. Starting as a regular secretary and then becoming the officer manager."

He noticed her nervousness and the tightly clasped hands. "You worked for which organization?"

"KGB," she whispered. Looking down at her folded hands she expected to have the meeting end…

"Then you are aware of the security precautions that are needed to safe guard information," he stated.

"Yes, I am." She raised her head looking at Dennis.

"You are aware that this is a security company?" Dennis inquired.

"Yes."

"Although we don't handle national secrets all the information we have on our clients is handled in the strictest of confidence," he paused. "Forgive me, please, for my lack of manners. Would you care for something to drink, I'm afraid all I can offer you at the moment is coffee or maybe a cold Pepsi."

"That's quite all right," she held up her hand. "Nothing for me thanks."

"May I call you Maria?" He was going on his gut feelings and his dire need for office experience.

"Yes," she agreed. "That will be fine."

"When can you start?"

She brightened excitedly. "Right now if you need me to."

"Welcome to Grady Security, Maria." He shook her hand. "Let me show you around."

Walking down the hall, he continued. "Right now we have six employees hired to monitor the security systems.

I am hoping to hire more any day now. Barney Baker is our installer and he is out on a job right now." He entered a door that was marked 'Employees Only'.

"These are the control panels. They are manned twenty-four hours a day. Until I can hire more people, they are working seven days a week. There are two people in here at all times. We also have at the present time, two contracts pending for onsite security guards." He escorted her back down the hall.

"Their schedule will eventually be your responsibility. All guards will have radio contact with the supervisor on watch here. Right now, there are no armed posts. They are planned for the future but that requires a ton of paper work and a training officer to ensure proper procedures are carried out. Here's your desk. There's an employee welcome packet in your desk. You'll find everything in there you need. I'll let you settle in. Make a list of any supplies you need that you can't find in the closet down the hall."

The next morning the phone rang. "Grady Security, one moment please."

"Dennis." Maria called on the intercom. "A Captain Daniels from the base."

"Jack," Dennis greeted. "What can I do for you?"

"Have a couple boys you might be interested in, can you be here at thirteen hundred?"

"Sure can, I was hoping you would call." He made a note on his desk calendar. "Have a contract hanging right now, I'm just waiting on warm bodies to fill the slot."

"I've looked over their records and both have received excellent reviews," Jack laughed. "Just can't convince their wives on how good a deal they're passing up."

"I'll see you at thirteen hundred." Dennis hung up and his stomach reminded him that he had skipped breakfast.

Just before noon, Dennis pulled into the parking lot of Gunny's Café. His palms were sweaty and it felt as if the tightness around his neck were a noose instead of a tie. He hadn't been in to see Rose in three weeks, seemed more like three years. One look at her smiling face erased the time completely. Just watching through the window his body responded physically to her. The smile that beamed a welcome message to all who entered, her hair bouncing around her shoulders as she turned her head. Dennis's fingers itched to play in her fiery tresses, to feel the creamy texture of her skin and the passion of her kiss.

Dennis opened the door and he tried to calm the nervous butterflies that fluttered inside.

"Hi. I…we, haven't seen you in a while. What brings you around now?"

"I have an appointment at Camp Lejeune this afternoon. Figured I would grab lunch first. This is still a café?" he teased. Inwardly Dennis hoped that she would soon be the main selection but for now, his fingers and other more intimate parts of his body would have to wait.

"Last time I checked Gunny was still cooking," she giggled. The tension between them was causing her to act like a teen talking to her first boy. *I actually giggled,* she thought. *Get a grip girl.*

"Have a seat." Even to her ears, it sounded like a sultry offer for sex rather than a seat in the café.

*Go for it! Step around the counter and ravish her mouth right now.* A little voice in Dennis's ear suggested. *Then carry her upstairs and be done with it.*

"Would you shut up?"

"Pardon me?"

At Debbie's startled expression, he realized he had spoken aloud.

"I'm sorry Debbie. I was talking to myself." Dennis ordered and waited. While he waited, he watched Rose from the corner of his eye. He felt a little smug as she kept glancing in his direction. One knee was bent and her toe was tapping out a nervous rhythm on the floor. He was so happy there was no way to hid his smile as she approached the table.

"Dennis, I want to thank you for the flowers and the earrings. You shouldn't have gone to such expense."

He had to admit; the golden rose was a work of art. Pinned to her ears they came to life. The ruby glowed in the light and the miniature jade leaves matched her eyes perfectly.

"I'm glad you like them. On you they look every bit as beautiful as I dreamed."

Feeling heat flush her body at the compliment, she turned away. "Thank you." A customer approached the counter. "Excuse me, back to work." She was thankful for the diversion.

Dennis felt a fresh wave of tenderness for Rose as he noticed the fuller breasts and extended waistline. She was beautiful.

"Hello Dennis," Gunny greeted with an outstretched hand. "How's your little project going?"

"Real good, Gunny. Better than expected for such a short time. Having Dad's support from the home office has been a big help."

"When are you going to tell Rose?"

Gunny had that 'concerned father' look of raised eyebrows, and tilted head. His tongue was in his upper lip making it appear he was chewing tobacco. Fingers lightly drummed on the table.

"Soon, Gunny," he promised. "Real soon."

So intensely aware of Dennis across the room, she lost track and had to start counting the change over again. Dropping a quarter it rolled on the floor, as if guided by an unseen hand, and stopped at Dennis's feet. Handing the customer another coin Rose went to retrieve the one she dropped.

Bending down to pick up the coin it was impossible not to notice the large bulge in Dennis's pants. Swallowing with difficulty Rose looked into his amused eyes. They were alight with a sensuous gleam. His lips twitched with an amused grin.

"You still have that effect Rose." He whispered just loud enough for her ears. "Why Rose, I do believe you are blushing."

When Dennis paid for his meal Rose tried to avoid his eyes. The touch of his hand on hers caused her to jump.

"A little edgy today or is it just me?" he challenged.

"You are terribly conceited if you think your being here has any effect on me." She was getting good at telling lies. At least they sounded good to her. After all, the only person Rose had to convince was herself.

"Not conceited," Dennis smiled. "Just observant."

* * * * *

Dennis's meeting at the base had been better than he had hoped for. Both marines jumped at the chance to stay in the Jacksonville area. Their children were in school; both their wives had local jobs. They would begin terminal leave in two weeks and be ready to start as his newest employees.

Going back to the office, he found a smaller version of his secretary at his desk. He smiled. "Hi there. How are you today?" She darted behind Maria and hid. Her Robin's egg blue eyes were wide with fright.

"Come Mihiela." She spoke in her native tongue. "This is Mr. Grady, my new employer."

"I'm afraid she hasn't learned much English yet," she apologized. "She has always been shy around strangers. In addition, the escape was very stressful. We were almost caught. When she becomes more adjusted, you won't keep her quiet. I hope it was all right to bring her here. I haven't found anyone for her to stay with after school."

"Relax Maria. You may bring her any time you need to. This old warehouse has enough space to keep a dozen kids exploring. If you need to, she can use an extra office for a play room."

He looked deep into Mihiela's eyes. The call of freedom had been so great that her family had been willing to sacrifice everything to gain it. He remembered Mark's letter to the Pastor, and his own oath as he entered the service. This was what it all boiled down to, the right for a person to choose how and where they wanted to live.

He cleared his throat of the sudden lump that had risen. "Call Jacksonville Mercedes and let them know we will have night guards available in two weeks."

"Your meeting on the base was successful," she concluded.

Dennis smiled. "Yes, very much so."

"Is—is there something you are not telling me?" she hesitated.

"What do you mean?"

"That smile is not about a business meeting at the base."

"Is that another specialty you have, smile reader?" he laughed easily.

"No, Nicoli is a passionate husband. I have seen that look many times. There is a special woman in you life?"

"Yes, there is a special woman," he admitted. "Hopefully, she will soon be in my life."

"Then, I will pray for your happiness."

* * * * *

Rose was in a quagmire. Watching the clock, waiting. She brushed her hair for the tenth time. Was he coming or not? She wished she knew. The magnetic attraction between them was still there. Judging by the state of nervous energy she had it was if possible even stronger. The best thing for her would be to forget and go on. If only it were that easy. All it had taken was one look, one smile, and all the self-denial lectures she had given herself went by the wayside. In his presence, the desire was almost tangible.

A gale force storm blew in from the Atlantic. Rain and sleet pelted the window. The wind howled and moaned around the building. It seemed as if the demons of hell had been turned loose to ride the storm, bringing Richard's words upon the wind to torment her. The howling mocked her desire. How long must she carry his bitterness? Would she ever stop hearing his abuse in her mind? Covering her head with her pillow Rose tried to muffle the accusing voices of the night.

The next morning Rose stood in front of the mirror. "Get a life girl," she lectured. "You can't afford to fall to pieces every time you and Dennis meet. Your life is cluttered enough as it is without more involvement with him. You have the café to think about and the baby." She automatically brushed her hair, her mind deep in thought.

She put down the hairbrush. "You owe Gunny. Where would you be if it wasn't for him and Maggie? What is he going to do without you? This is where you belong. With someone who appreciates and needs you."

Rose went downstairs and stepped into the café. The Rose who received the lecture must have stayed upstairs, because the one in the café fell like a moth singed in a flame. Dennis sat at the counter laughing with Gunny as if it were a normal everyday occurrence.

Dennis turned toward her and flashed her a smile. Her palms turned damp and her heart pounded like a drum in her chest. That couldn't be a normal 'Hi, how you doing!' smile. That type of smile didn't leave your knees weak and put a burning in the pit of your stomach.

"Figured you would be gone by now?" Rose fussed with the coffee cups. Straightening what didn't need straightened. She checked the menus that had already been checked a dozen times before. Anything to keep from watching the muscles move under the material stretched across his shoulders. His hair was windblown, reminding her of the days on the river where their only concern was catching the next meal or where to make love.

"Nope, still here," he gave Gunny a wink. "Thought you might like to go out tonight and eat." He watched the stack of saucers in her hands slip. Trying to correct the movement Rose sent them crashing to the floor.

"Now see what you made me do!" she exclaimed. Broken pieces of the saucers were scattered across the floor. She bent down to begin picking up the bigger pieces.

He looked at Gunny in confusion. Gunny was having all he could do to keep from laughing.

"What did I do?"

Gunny waved him away and went into the kitchen. No longer able to contain himself he leaned against the island table and laughed until the tears trickled down his cheeks.

"All I did was ask if you wanted to go out tonight. You were the one who dropped the dishes," he rationalized.

"You could have given me some warning. It took me by surprise." She swept the floor collecting the small fragments in the dustpan.

"Okay, the surprise is over. You still haven't answered my question. Would you like to go out to dinner?" he repeated. "A simple yes, or no will be sufficient."

"Dennis, as much as I want to I don't think it would be a good idea."

"What's wrong Rose, with us going out to eat. We both have to eat. Why can't we enjoy the evening together. We are still family. You have made it clear that what ever was between us on the river had to end," he reminded her. "I am asking to take my brother's wife out to dinner. That's all."

Rose spotted a small piece that had been missed by the broom. Stalling in giving him an answer, she squatted and picked up the fragment. "What time?"

*Yes*! Dennis wanted to get on the counter and do a happy jig. Instead he calmly announced. "I'll pick you up at seven if that's convenient?"

"Seven o'clock it is." She went to greet a customer, all to aware that his eyes followed her every movement.

She might be able to deny wanting to go to dinner with Dennis to his face, and to others, but not to herself…there was nothing she wanted more. Going out with Dennis rated right up alongside playing with sharp knives or matches. Eventually you were either going to cut yourself or be burned.

His brand permanently marked her already. When they were on the river, she had been burned. With Mark's death tearing a hole in her, leaving Nashville had cut deep into what heart she had left. Thinking, she could fit into his world would only open herself up for more heartache. If all she was destined to have were memories then starting tonight, she would grab every opportunity to make more.

# Chapter Sixteen

Doing the books that afternoon, the figures wouldn't add up. After tabulating the same column three times, and getting three different answers, she closed the books, and daydreamed of lazy warm days on a small sandy beach somewhere on the Cumberland River.

Feeling alive with renewed energy, she hurried up the stairs. Hurrying through a quick shower, she dressed and waited. Ready to go to dinner, or anywhere else tonight as long as the need inside her was filled.

With her expanding waistline, she was thankful for having bought a bigger dress. She finished a last minute brush of her hair, and checked to ensure her straps weren't showing. Six months ago, she could have gotten by just fine without the constraining undergarment, but not now.

The buzzer sounded and she turned away from the mirror and headed down the stairs.

Rose took one look at Dennis in his expensive dark gray suit and light blue shirt. She knew she wasn't dressed for wherever it was Dennis planned on going.

"You look lovely tonight Rose," he complimented her.

"Thank you. You look great too." If he thought she looked lovely, who was she to argue?

Dennis held her door and then got in.

"How was your meeting at the base?"

"It went really well. I hired a couple of marines who were getting out soon."

"A long way to come just to hire a couple of men," she declared.

"Their prior training makes the effort worthwhile." Dennis hedged his true purpose for being in Jacksonville.

Dennis pulled into the parking lot and Rose's good spirits wilted. "Dennis!" she exclaimed. "No Dennis, not tonight. We can't eat here."

"Why not?" He noticed the panic in her voice. "This is the best restaurant in the city. I like to never got reservations on such a short notice."

"That's precisely why we can't eat here." She slumped back against the seat. *This is why we will never make it together, I eat hamburgers, and he eats filet mignon.* She turned to look pleadingly at Dennis. "I'm not dressed to eat here."

Dennis got out and came around to open her door. Holding out his hand, he waited.

"Dennis!"

"I have reservations Rose."

Reluctantly she got out of the car. "This is embarrassing," she whispered.

"Rose dear," he cupped her chin and kissed her forehead, "your beauty will make every other woman here pale in comparison. Besides, you stated that you didn't get embarrassed, if I remember correctly."

"Now is not the time for jokes, Dennis. I knew this was going to be a bad evening as soon as I saw your suit and tie." She started for the entrance. "Well, do I have to eat alone?"

Rose checked her coat at the door. When hung beside the minks and furs, hers looked out of place and shabby. She watched the glances of the other dinners as they were escorted to the table.

Dennis gave her a knowing smile. "See, they can't keep their eyes from following your every move."

"They are probably just wondering why such a handsome man is burdened with a woman so plain and unfashionably dressed."

"Is that how you see yourself Rose? Plain, as in ordinary, average, and run of the mill?" He stifled a laugh. "If it is, then let me open your eyes for you to the way other people see you.

"The color of your hair, the way it shimmers in the light. It's almost like flames of fire dancing around your face. Your eyes, sparkle like emeralds in the sea, alive with passion and the love of life. When you smile, the sun need not shine for it can brighten even an old man's heart. If the rest of you were built like Twiggy, which I assure you is not the case. You would still turn heads wherever you go."

Rose was amazed, he saw her in this manner. She looked into his eyes and felt humbled. Unable to speak, she watched as he lifted her hand and kissed it. To her further amazement, he continued holding her hand even though the waiter arrived to take their order.

The warmth of his hand seemed to travel up her arm and spread. She was powerless to break the spell that bonded them together.

"So, how long are you going to be in Jacksonville," she inquired.

"I'm not really sure, depends on a couple of things." Dennis intentionally kept his answer vague.

"You can't or won't be more specific," she pried further.

"Yes to both," he laughed. "Something has come up that may require my presence for…a few days more."

A few days could be as few as two or as many as a week. However long she had, she would build as many memories as she could to carry her through the lonely years ahead.

The food was superb. Her filet, cooked to perfection, melted in her mouth. She licked her lips of the savory juice and watched as Dennis's eyes widened in a different type of hunger.

Dennis hardly tasted his food. It could have been burnt clear through and he wouldn't have noticed.

The evening was wonderful, for Rose it was proving exceedingly optimistic to end with Dennis in her bed. With the touches during dinner, the warmth of being in his arms on the dance floor feeling his hardness as he held her only made her own desire more noticeable, more demanding to be filled. By the time Dennis reached the café, she wanted him with such intensity that it frightened her.

Escorting Rose to the door, knowing by her sultry voice and luminous eyes that if he walked upstairs, he could have a little bit of heaven on earth in her arms made his decision that much harder. He stooped and she met him half way. A quick kiss that only fanned the coals of desire, making them hotter.

Dennis opened the door.

"Goodnight Rose," he whispered. "Thank you so much for going out to dinner with me." He wanted a future with Rose, not just one or two nights of memories, and he was determined to wait until he could have it all.

Confused and deflated like a burst balloon, Rose stepped through the door. The door closed behind her and she sat down on the steps.

"Damn you," she swore. Gunny's words came back to her, "You sent him away." She slowly climbed the stairs, undressed, and went to bed.

By morning, the unfulfilled desire had gone through the transformation of frustration to anger. Angry with Dennis, at herself, and the world in general, she slammed he door. With not having the cause of her resentment handy to vent her frustrations and anger on, Rose went to work with both barrels fully primed.

Gunny was about ready to call out to her when he noticed the tightness in her smile and the fire in her eyes.

Walking over to the large table where locals gathered in the mornings for coffee she noticed the sugar container was low. Slamming the container on the table, she looked around and found the unsuspecting Debbie nearby.

"Just what have you been doing this morning?" she demanded. "This place isn't ready for customers. You know better than that, Debbie. Every morning these are supposed to be checked and filled. Especially this table, cream, and sugar run out fast enough in the morning without having the day started low. Do I have to do everything myself?"

"Give it a break girl," Debbie fired back. "The new girl hasn't shown up yet. I'll get to it. Why don't you park it for a while 'til you calm down or else grab a service tray and lend a hand?" She continued working as Rose glared coldly at her.

"You can't talk to me that way," she threatened.

"I just did..."

"Rose!" Gunny bellowed from the kitchen. "In the office."

"I'll be there in a couple of minutes Gunny."

"Now!"

Gunny waited impatiently for Rose to arrive in the office.

She walked in and closed the door.

"Rose dear, would you tell me what all that was all about?"

"She wasn't getting things done," she accused. "She knows what has to be done first thing in the mornings."

"This has nothing to do with the sugar and cream on the table, Rose. You haven't acted like this since before my Maggie died. We have all forgotten things out front. Have I ever chewed on you and yelled the way you were just doing?"

When she didn't answer, he raised his voice in frustration. "Well, have I?"

"No," she whispered.

"I think this has more to do with Dennis, than anything else." He stood looking at her and shook his head. "Listen, girl, you just don't walk away from someone and tell them it's over and then expect the next time you see him that everything will be cozy and pick up where you left off," he paused for breath. "I know you two got close that week that things were upside down. You were the one who walked away."

"You don't have to keep reminding me, okay!" Angrily she turned and stared out the back window.

"Sorry, Gunny. I guess I have been a little short with everyone lately. Just so many things have happened lately. I am trying to sort it all out."

Gunny approached and placed his hands on her shoulders and gently turned her around. "Just give it some time. Don't rush through this life without taking the time to enjoy it. I would rather have your smiling face and cheerful warm self out front than all the full sugar and cream containers in the world."

Rose gave Gunny a big hug.

"You know, I love you, Rose."

"I love you too, Gunny." She reached up and kissed his cheek. "Don't let the customers see the tears in your eyes Gunny, it will spoil that hardboiled marine image of yours." She laughed as he went out the door.

"Debbie, sorry for being such a bitch earlier."

"Well you're pregnant so it can't be PMS so the next guess would be sexual tension. You and Dennis not getting along?"

"What are you, Mother Teresa and I have to give you my confession," she teased. "For your information we are getting along just fine, I couldn't ask for a finer brother-in-law."

"It's gone back to being a brother-in-law now, and whose fault is that?" she asked knowingly.

"That's all it has ever been."

"Rose," she admonished, "you're full of it. Come on we have ten minutes before the doors open."

* * * * *

Reaching the office that morning Maria had the coffee going. "Maria, you are going to spoil me. What is on the schedule for today?"

Maria went down the list.

"Jay's Gold Jewelry called. They want to talk about updating their alarm system."

"Westside Engineering called. They are interested in us giving them an estimate on a new bank's security system.

"There are two more applicants coming in this morning from the employment office. The one for the guard position has prior experience with a reputable company and the other one who applied for the control room position was in the navy. His navy position was," she double checked the application, "Operations Supervisor on the USS Saratoga."

"I know the boys in there will be grateful for a break," he stated.

"Also," she went on. "Sylvester O'Toul would like you to stop by tonight. He said it was important."

"Gunny didn't say what it was about?" he questioned.

"Just said it was important and he didn't want to discuss it over the phone," she clarified. "However, I did notice a nervousness in his voice.

"The realtor called, a house like you are wanting might be on the market in a week or two. She wanted to give you a head's up on it.

"I checked with Barney, and he will be free by one o'clock." She finished the day's calendar and waited.

Dennis calculated the time they would need at the engineers' office. "Call Westside and let them know that one o'clock is fine. Remind Barney, when he gets wrapped up in his little black boxes, time is not a relative factor. The only thing that will be noticed is an empty cup and a full bladder."

"What about Jay's Jewelry?" she asked.

"Make an appointment for tomorrow morning." he made a mental note for himself. Get in touch with ..."

"Barney and let him know," she finished.

"Anything happen last night in the control room?" He gave a quick glance at the logs.

"Nothing out of the ordinary," she informed him.

"Thank you Maria. That will be all for now." He set the control room logs down and picked up an estimate for another installation.

"How is Nicoli doing with his schooling?" He spoke before she left the room. Maria turned around with a smile on her face.

"He is doing great, thank you. The college is trying to accelerate him in his classes." She went to her desk thankful for such a thoughtful boss. Maria thought back to the State Security Office in Romania. The strict rules and severe punishments if a rule was broken or even bent, their total lack of concern for family matters. The state came first and last with nothing in-between. Romania was their only thought. Her home had been turned into a slave state. She hated President Ceausescu and the Communists with their constant watching and listening to everything. All it took was one harsh word or critical comment and the person was in jail.

The outer door opened bringing Maria back from her past.

"I'm Timothy Moore. I had a nine o'clock appointment."

"One moment please while I let Mr. Grady know you are here." She called Dennis on the intercom. "Sir, your nine o'clock appointment is here."

Gunny kept checking the package he had for Dennis. He couldn't get here soon enough to suit Gunny. He might be on a wild goose chase, but he wasn't taking any chances. The package was going to remain closed until Dennis arrived.

At two o'clock, Gunny went across the alley to the home he had shared with Maggie for so many years. He picked up a bottle and two glasses, settled in his favorite chair on the front porch, and laid his pistol within reach.

Dennis finished with Westside Engineers at three o'clock. Barney was headed back to the office. He had two weeks to develop an estimate. With what they were wanting, two weeks was going to be putting a rush on the schedule. Grady Security was a last minute consideration. Westside wasn't impressed with the other two companies that had put bids in. Barney assured him that by the time he finished they would be impressed.

At three forty-five Dennis pulled up to Gunny's home.

Walking up to the house, he noticed the unopened bottle of Chivas Regal and the butt plate of a 45. Gunny kicked a chair out for him.

"Care to join me?" Without waiting for an answer, he opened the bottle and poured a couple of shots into each glass.

Picking up his glass he swirled the amber liquid. "Here is to better days Dennis. We're all about due." Thus said, he raised his glass to Dennis's and clinked them together.

They each took a sip; Dennis's curiosity forced him to speak. "What are we celebrating?"

Gunny reached down beside his chair and set a brown paper sack on the table. "Go ahead," he offered. "It won't bite."

Dennis set his glass down and took the sack. Looking inside, he was puzzled. "What's this? Some kind of joke." He emptied the bag.

Gunny took another sip from his glass and stared at the doll sitting on the table.

"Just a little over four years ago on a chilly, rainy night I took the trash out to the dumpster. There was a young girl in the dumpster eating scraps of food thrown out after the evening dinner hour. She was wearing rags and dirty. She finally came up on the porch after I promised her some good food. My Maggie, took to her right off. Still don't know how she managed it, but she got the girl into the house and gave her a bath. You should have heard the fuss'en and cuss'en that went on. After washing her hair a half-a-dozen times to get it clean we discovered a precious little rose that had been hidden too long among the weeds." He paused to take another shallow sip.

Dennis watched the emotions play across his face as he mentioned his wife, the change in his voice and the softness in his eyes. Gunny had that far away look, reliving the memory.

Gunny continued, "The night we found Rose, she was clinging to that doll. That's what most of the cuss'en was about. In order to take a bath she had to put the doll down.

We finally convinced her that she could hide the doll wherever she wanted so that when she decided to leave all she had to do was get her doll and go.

"I don't know if she remembers or not. Couldn't even guess. That night when Agent Rodgers was here, reminded me of the doll. I hadn't seen it for so long I wasn't sure it was still here. I looked for it for several days and gave up. Found it late last night, by accident, down in the basement."

"Why didn't you just ask Rose?" Dennis picked up the doll.

"With what she has been through." He poured a small amount of whiskey in his glass and slowly shook his head. "I didn't want to stir up the ashes of bad memories. It may or may not hold the missing material. It may just be what's left of the few good childhood memories she has."

The doll had seen better days. The cloth was worn and dirty. Three years of accumulated dust hadn't helped its condition. Dennis carefully inspected the doll.

"Do you have a magnifying glass Gunny?"

"There should be one in the house somewhere. Maggie hated wearing glasses and used a big handheld magnifier to read." He got up slowly and after several minutes returned with the magnifying glass in hand.

Dennis checked every thread of the doll. It wasn't until his second inspection that he noticed the minute variation in the threads. Pulling a small penknife from his pocket, he cut the thread. Slowly, the hole in the doll grew bigger. When he had opened the seam about three inches, he felt around inside. His fingers brushed against a small object. Dennis pulled out what appeared to be a waterproof container the size of a cigarette.

"Look what we have here!"

"Just what are we looking at?" Gunny moved his chair closer.

"This is a standard CIA issue microfilm transporter. Completely waterproof, it can be hidden anywhere indefinably. Even in body cavities. Its time to call Agent Rodgers, I think we just found his missing documents."

Four hours later, a car pulled up, Agent Rodgers and two other men got out. All three men approached the house.

"Dennis, Gunny," Rodgers made the introductions. "This is Agent Hamilton and Agent Gregory. May I see the package?"

Dennis handed over the small cylinder.

"The seal is unbroken. Aren't you a little curious as to what is inside?" Rodgers took out a knife and slit the seal. Separating the two halves revealed a rolled up strip of film. He motioned to Agent Gregory who went to the car and retrieved a briefcase. Rodgers opened the case and inserted the film into a small reader. Hamilton and Gregory both glanced at the screen and nodded in confirmation.

Rodgers took the film. Lighting a match he touched the flame to the film. When the flame reached for his fingers, he dropped the destroyed film in the dirt. The flames flickered and died as the last of the film burned.

"Thanks to you, the CIA implants into communist governments around the world can sleep in relative peace for the first time in four years. They have been living in fear that one day that film would fall into the wrong hands and they would be arrested and killed. We owe you a debt of gratitude."

"Gunny," Rose called out. "Is everything all right?"

"Yes dear, come on up."

"Hello Rose, I just got your message the other day." Rogers explained. "I have been out of touch for a while."

"Dad," Rose shyly approached.

Thomas Rodgers, a man who had been hardened by years of field investigations, and espionage opened his arms and embraced his daughter. Together they wept tears of happiness.

Dennis looked at Gunny and noticed even he had tears on his face.

Holding one arm around his daughter, Rodgers held out his hand to Dennis. The old animosity toward the CIA was still present, but his mistrust of Rodgers disappeared as he watched Rose bury her past and accept his love.

"Rose," he whispered, "I have to go back tonight. The plane is waiting at the airport. Just as soon as possible, I'll get back down." He kissed the top of her head. "I have always loved you.

"By the way Dennis, Congratulations!" Agent Rodgers turned as he got to the car. "I hear your office here in Jacksonville is really taking off."

Rose watched the car drive away. She spun around and bristled. "What new office is he talking about? What is my old doll doing out here ripped open? Somebody had better start answering some questions," she demanded.

"I found your old doll last night in the basement," explained Gunny. "I remembered Rodgers asking about anything you had brought with you."

"Did that give you any right to destroy it without asking me first!" she raged.

"Rose," Dennis injected. "It is not ruined. I opened the seam in the same place as before."

"Now I know you're both nuts," she raised her arms in unbelief. "Although it is dirty and seen better days, it had never been torn or sewed before. I suppose now you are going to tell me that you found the documents the CIA was looking for inside the doll."

"Well as a matter of fact Rose, we did," Dennis stated. "Rodgers flew all the way down here to verify the documents and then personally insure their destruction. What's left is a pile of burnt film."

"What was it, some Senator's girl friend list or some other garbage? Do you really expect me to believe that for all these years Top Secret documents have been in my old doll? That the doll Mother gave me just after Richard left, the doll that I carried on the streets for a year in an old worn out suitcase, carried microfilm?"

"Rose, the microfilm was a list of agents around the world."

She sat down heavily on the steps.

Dennis hoped that with this information, if he were lucky, she wouldn't bring up the other question. Inside, he was worried that it wasn't time to spring the big surprise.

"Now that I'm sitting you might as well tell me about the business thing. When were you going to tell me you opened an office here? Or were you?" She looked up into his face.

*So much for luck.*

"When I was sure it would work. Just as soon as I had built up a solid client base." Dennis watched as she hung her head. Crimson tendrils of hair hid her face.

"Why here?" She spoke so softly that Dennis had to sit down beside her to hear.

"Why pick Jacksonville, North Carolina, for an office? Out of fifty states and thousands of large cities why pick here?

"I suppose you knew about this too?" She turned and looked accusingly at Gunny. The silence was so loud it hurt.

"I am waiting for an explanation. Why have you been hiding it from me? Am I the only one in town that doesn't know about it?" Standing up she continued. "I'm going, when you decide to let me know, I'll be in my apartment."

"Rose," he pleaded.

She stopped but didn't turn around.

"I opened a new office here because I realized that…"

"That what Dennis?" She held her breath without realizing it. Her heart strained to hear the words that would make her life complete.

Dennis continued, "That living in Nashville without you was impossible. I know how important the café is to you. I discussed it with Dad, and he agreed we should give it a try.

"Just when did you come to this decision Dennis?" Rose couldn't believe what he was saying. It was like a dream come true. Like the legend of the Phoenix rising out of the ashes, her heart took on new hope.

"I was miserable at home. Mother and I would argue over the simplest things. When I saw the news about Richard I knew I had to come, if for no other reason than the dream."

"What dream?" She turned to face him, could it be he had being plagued by the same nightmares as she.

"Right after I met you I had a dream, about Mark. Crimson tongues of fire surrounded him and he was holding an emerald. He kept trying to hand the jewel to me, but I wouldn't take it." Dennis raked his fingers through his hair.

"The second dream came when I was asleep on your couch. Only this time at the end of the dream, I was holding the emerald and surrounded by the fire. When I woke up I was holding your arms."

"I had a dream," she whispered. "The night Mark died. He said, "Remember I love you." I reached for him but couldn't touch him. That's why I knew for certain that he was dead when I saw the news that morning."

"Were they just dreams or were they real?" Dennis pondered.

"My mother and her mother had the dreams. Not often. But when they did they always came true." Rose remembered her mother's dream of the hardship that Rose would have to face. Then Carmen's face had glowed, "Rose hold on, there will be happiness in the end." Those were the last words her mother had spoke.

"Rose, I love you. I don't want to spend another moment without you in my life. Will you do me the honor of being my wife?"

Rose felt her heart would burst with joy. "Yes! Oh Yes!"

She threw herself into his arms and passionately kissed him. "I love you, Dennis Grady. I have fought it from the very start, and lost the fight. I am so glad, I can follow my heart and honestly say it."

"Say it again, Rose."

"I love you, Dennis."

Gunny felt the tears running down his face. "This calls for a toast." He raised his glass.

"To Dennis, and his Crimson Rose."

# Chapter Seventeen

That next Saturday dawned chilly but bright with a cloudless sky. Rose was sitting at the cash register when the door opened and Thomas Rodgers walked in.

"Morning Rose."

"Dad! What a pleasant surprise." She slipped off the chair and slid her large bulk around the edge of the counter.

"You look lovely this morning," he complimented. "Congratulations on the engagement. Thank you for calling and letting me know."

"Dad, I know exactly how I look. Fat." Rose gave him a hug. "I am afraid that this wedding may be a little unconventional. I plan on both you and Gunny giving me away." Together they made their way to a booth near the register.

"I took a couple of weeks leave." Thomas looked up at the waitress. "Coffee, please. I was hoping to be able to spend some time in the evenings and get acquainted with my daughter, before she got married."

"That would be wonderful Dad." The word was coming easier to her lips every time she said it.

"I have so much time on the book, I had to use it or loose it. I couldn't think of a place I would rather be, than here with you." He picked up the cup that the waitress set down and took a sip.

"Sundays are pretty slow around here. We close at two and all day on Monday. Dennis will be by later this evening. We could all go out and eat." She remembered the animosity Dennis showed the first time they had met.

"He doesn't have anything against you Thomas. It's the agency itself, and the way they used to do things."

"Well, in some cases they haven't changed very much." He patted her hand. "I'm sure we can work out our differences."

The door opened and Rose looked up. "Morning Sheala, Please join us. Sheala this is my Dad, the real one," she laughed. "Thomas Rodgers. Dad, this is Sheala Rosenthal."

Thomas stood up and shook hands with her. Rose noticed that the handshake went on a little longer than required. When they sat down Rose continued.

"Sheala is my OB/GYN Doctor at the base. She has really helped me since Mark's death."

"I want to thank you for taking such good care of my daughter. Not having been around, I'm glad that someone has been looking after her." Thomas held Rose's hand, trying to regain some of the closeness that was missed over the years.

"It has been my pleasure," Sheala said. "We have grown very close over the months she has been coming to see me. We share a number of things together despite the obvious differences. The reason I stopped by, I have decided that it's time to retire. I made the selection for Commander..."

"Congratulations Sheala." Rose hugged her. "I am happy for you. What's this about retiring?"

"Well it won't be for a while. I'll have to stay in for another year," she acknowledged. "However, I have decided to go into private practice. I plan to open an office here in Jacksonville."

"That's even better yet!" exclaimed Rose. "Even after you get out, you can be my Doctor."

"With all this celebration I might as well add my news," Thomas interjected. "I have over twenty years of service with the agency, and I too plan on retiring. Only it isn't going to take a year to do."

"What are you going to do Dad?" Rose asked. "All these years of cloak and dagger with the agency. I just can't see you sitting behind a desk somewhere or on a boat, fishing for the rest of our life. You're not that old."

Thomas chuckled and then broke out a big smile that was directed not at Rose but at Sheala. "Already, she is telling me what I shouldn't be doing when I retire."

"Rose, that's another reason why I am here. Not the main reason, but part of it. Dennis called. He needs someone to help run the operations of the company here. Frank has taken over the training but Dennis needs someone who is willing to travel more, recruiting employees and more clients. He asked me to consider it."

"And." Rose sat impatiently waiting for his answer.

"If Dennis is still willing, I'll put in the retirement papers when I get back."

"This calls for a celebration. Sheala we are going out to dinner tonight, won't you join us?" Rose invited.

"Thank you but no," Sheala declined. "I wouldn't want to intrude."

"You wouldn't be intruding, unless your husband would object?" Thomas noticed the absence of a ring and hoped, at least for tonight that it also meant the absence of a husband.

"There isn't any husband to object, I'm divorced," she stated. "He didn't like being moved every few years or the living overseas. I think what he really didn't like was being called a dependent."

"Then there is no reason you can't go to dinner with us," Rose reasoned.

"Please, come with us." Thomas looked hopefully at Sheala. "If you don't, I will be the odd man out at dinner. You can be my date."

"Well, I…," she hesitated. "All right, I accept." There was something about Thomas that intrigued her. Was it the life he had led? She didn't think that was it. She had known plenty of men in the service who led dangerous lives. None had ever appealed to her for that reason. The connection she felt when they shook hands was worth checking out.

## Chapter Eighteen

The wedding was held on a blustery day in March, at the Camp Lejeune Base Chapel. With Gunny on one side and Thomas Rodgers on the other, they walked Rose down the aisle. Her wedding dress, an off white satin covered with a white mesh, sparkled from hundreds of tiny pearls that caught and reflected the light.

William and Shalinn were there along with Pete and most of the regular customers of the café. Frank the Ferret was standing as best man. Debbie was standing as her Maid-of-Honor. Seven-year-old Mihiela DuBre, scattered rose petals in the aisle

When they reached the front of the chapel, the Chaplin asked.

"Who give'th this woman?

Gunny and Thomas Rodgers spoke at the same time.

"We do." They each kissed a cheek and handed her over to Dennis.

Rose felt a healthy kick and winced. A strong ache spread across her lower back.

Thomas Rodgers went to the pew, stepped in beside newly promoted Commander Sheala Rosenthal, and gave her hand a squeeze.

"Shall we pray? Lord, we thank You for the love that Dennis and Rose share. That this love has risen out of tragedy bears witness that the human spirit can rise out of despair, and love will triumph in the end. May the vows that are spoken here today, be recorded on the walls of heaven. Lord, may they receive strength and grace today, and each day they share together in the years to come. Amen."

The Chaplin looked compassionately at Rose and then glanced down at her huge waistline.

"Today we are gathered together in the sight of God and these witnesses to join William Dennis Grady and Rose Ann Grady in holy matrimony.

"Do you Dennis, take Rose to be your lawfully wedded wife? To love, honor and cherish? Do you pledge yourself to her in sickness and in health, for richer, for poorer, forsaking all others for as long as you both shall live?"

"I do."

"Do you Rose, take Dennis to be your lawfully wedded husband? To love, honor and cherish? Do you pledge yourself to him in sickness and in health, for richer, for poorer, forsaking all others for as long as you both shall live?"

"I do."

Dennis and Rose turned to face each other. Together they spoke. "With this Ring as a token and pledge of my love for you, I thee wed."

"By the power vested in me by God, and the State of North Carolina," the Chaplin placed his hand on theirs, "I now pronounce you husband and wife. What God hath joined together let no man put asunder."

The Chaplin smothered a smile as Rose's wedding dress, taunt over her waist, moved.

"Dennis, you may kiss your Bride."

He pulled Rose into his arms and kissed her. There was a solid kick at his waistline. He looked questionable at Rose.

Rose had felt the last several kicks. This one was definitely stronger than the last. She smiled at Dennis. "I think, he is happy too."

The Chaplin turned them to face those that had gathered. "I present to you, Mr. and Mrs. Dennis Grady."

Dennis and Rose left the church through a shower of rice and rose petals. Marines from Mark's division, all survivors of the Beirut Bombing raised their sabers to form an arch.

Rose swore she heard Mark's voice.

She answered, "Semper Fi"

* * * * *

Dennis opened the car door for Rose. They were headed back to Gunny's for the reception.

Rose started to step into the car when pain shot through her like a hot knife. Doubling over, she clutched at the door for support. Almost instantly, water flowed down her legs soaking her dress. Dennis reached for her, and she clung to him in desperation.

"Her water broke," Sheala announced. She laid her hand on Rose's shoulder. "Not many people get married and have a baby on the same day. We need to get her to the hospital Dennis. There may not be time to get an ambulance here. I'll have the police give us an escort."

Commander Rosenthal went over to the Military Police Officer and explained the change of plans.

Sheala climbed into the back seat with Rose. "Go!"

Twenty minutes later Mark Sylvester Grady weighed in at six pounds, seven and three-quarter ounces. Turned upside down and swatted on his butt, Mark made his own announcement of his arrival into the world with a strong voice of disapproval.

The Wedding Celebration was moved with special permission from Gunny's to the hospital cafeteria. Proud Grandparents wearing jubilant smiles stood around the cake. Dennis and Rose were enjoying a moment of privacy in her room before he wheeled her downstairs to share in the cutting of the cake.

"Ahh, my sweet Rose." He leaned over and kissed her. "You are glowing in radiant beauty. Motherhood agrees with you."

Dennis gave her another kiss. "I have a surprise for you. You remember the yacht we borrowed. The owner decided to sell it. It's our wedding present from Dad and Mom. I renamed it."

Rose looked unbelieving at Dennis. "It's ours! It's really ours! Why would you rename it? What…"

"I named it after you."

"The Crimson Rose".

# Epilogue

The morning sky was turning gray as Rose Grady turned back the covers. Turning on the light she looked admirably at the sleeping form of her husband. After ten years of marriage, she still enjoyed looking at him. Placing a kiss on his bare shoulder, she felt his fingers slide seductively up her leg.

"Later love, when we have more time. We need to get ready." Rose swung her feet to the floor and padded to the bathroom.

Dennis watched the sensuous sway of her bare hips and the wind of desire rekindled the flames that had all but consumed them the night before.

"I'll get Mark up and dressed." Dennis climbed from the bed and belted on a robe.

Rose finished her shower and somehow managed to get the family out of the house on time.

At the Beirut Memorial, a large throng of people stood reverently silent in the early morning hours of October 22, 1993. The scent of the pine trees drifted in the early morning breeze. The Bradford pear trees that had been planted as part of the memorial, and the stately oaks were dressed in their fall splendor of red, orange, and yellow hues. Gray skies turned to blue, streaked with pale red and purple. Somewhere up in the trees birds were beginning the morning ritual of greeting the new day with a song. The noise from the street seemed to disappear as those gathered remembered lost loved ones and friends.

Rose approached the granite wall where the names of the 273 Americans, who died in Beirut and Grenada, were engraved. The bronze statue of a marine stood on the wall, keeping an eternal watch over his fallen brothers. Rose held the hand of nine-year-old Mark Sylvester, her eyes diligently searched for Mark's name. Running her fingers over the engraved letters, she turned and looked at Dennis.

He stood on the edge of the crowd holding the hand of six-year-old William Dennis the Third. Curled up in his other arm was thirteen-month-old Angelica Jade. The look of love and compassion on his face brought a tear to her eye as she turned back to the monument. Kissing her fingers, she ran them over Mark's name. Tears cascaded down her face as she knelt beside Mark's son and whispered in his ear. He stepped forward and laid a single pale red rose among the flowers already there.

Closing her eyes, Rose opened her heart.

*Oh Mark, although you're not here beside me, every time I look into our son's face, I see you. You would be so proud of him. I think he is going to be a marine just like you. If he wants to follow your dream I pray that you will watch over him when I can't.*

*Dennis and I are happy. His love and strength have always been there for me. I love him and our children dearly. The years have gone so quickly since you were taken from me, seems as though our love was but a fleeting whisper in the night. Yet your words, 'Remember I love you' echo still in the chambers of my mind and in my heart."*

She whispered, "I do, and always will."

# The Beirut Memorial

*'They Came in Peace'*

Dedicated in 1986, this graceful monument pays homage to the 273 Marines, Soldiers, and Sailors who died in the service of their nation in Beirut, Lebanon, and during the Grenada invasion. Names of the deceased are engraved on gray granite walls set in a placid grove of Carolina pines and azaleas. A bronze statue of a marine stands in an eternal vigil over his comrades, facing the NC Veterans' Cemetery Chapel. Funded entirely by donations of private citizens and businesses, the Memorial has become one of the most important destinations for visitors to Onslow County and Camp Lejeune.

Complementing the Memorial are 273 Bradford pear trees, one for each service member honored, planted along

Lejeune Boulevard (NC 24) from the Memorial to the Main Gate of Camp Lejeune. The Memorial is maintained by a joint USMC and civilian Beirut Memorial Advisory Board which sponsors an annual memorial service every October 23rd. Further information concerning the Memorial may be obtained at the Camp Lejeune Visitors Center (Building 812) near the Main Gate and the Onslow County Tourism Office at 1 Marine Boulevard (US 17).

## About the author:

Romance Author, R Casteel, retired from the US Navy in 1990. He enjoys the outdoors, loves to Scuba Dive, and is a Search and Rescue Diver. With twenty years of military service, which included experience as flight crewman, search and rescue, and four years as a Military Police Officer, it is of little wonder that his books are filled with suspense and intrigue.

As to his ability to write romance, Gloria for Best Reviews writes "I had thought Leigh Greenwood was the only man who wrote wonderful romance...I was wrong...Rod Casteel is right there too!"

Mr. Casteel lives in his hometown of Lancaster, Missouri and would love to hear from you.

R. Casteel welcomes mail from readers. You can write to them c/o Ellora's Cave Publishing at P.O. Box 787, Hudson, Ohio 44236-0787.

## Also by R. Casteel:

Mistress Of Table Rock

Tanieka: Daughter Of The Wolf

Texas Thunder

The Toymaker

# Why an electronic book?

We live in the Information Age—an exciting time in the history of human civilization in which technology rules supreme and continues to progress in leaps and bounds every minute of every hour of every day. For a multitude of reasons, more and more avid literary fans are opting to purchase e-books instead of paperbacks. The question to those not yet initiated to the world of electronic reading is simply: *why?*

1. *Price.* An electronic title at Ellora's Cave Publishing runs anywhere from 40-75% less than the cover price of the exact same title in paperback format. Why? Cold mathematics. It is less expensive to publish an e-book than it is to publish a paperback, so the savings are passed along to the consumer.
2. *Space.* Running out of room to house your paperback books? That is one worry you will never have with electronic novels. For a low one-time cost, you can purchase a handheld computer designed specifically for e-reading purposes. Many e-readers are larger than the average handheld, giving you plenty of screen room. Better yet, hundreds of titles can be stored within your new library—a single microchip. (Please note that Ellora's Cave does not endorse any specific brands. You can check our website at www.ellorascave.com for customer recommendations we make available to new consumers.)

3. *Mobility.* Because your new library now consists of only a microchip, your entire cache of books can be taken with you wherever you go.
4. *Personal preferences are accounted for.* Are the words you are currently reading too small? Too large? Too...**ANNOYING**? Paperback books cannot be modified according to personal preferences, but e-books can.
5. *Innovation.* The way you read a book is not the only advancement the Information Age has gifted the literary community with. There is also the factor of what you can read. Ellora's Cave Publishing will be introducing a new line of interactive titles that are available in e-book format only.
6. *Instant gratification.* Is it the middle of the night and all the bookstores are closed? Are you tired of waiting days—sometimes weeks—for online and offline bookstores to ship the novels you bought? Ellora's Cave Publishing sells instantaneous downloads 24 hours a day, 7 days a week, 365 days a year. Our e-book delivery system is 100% automated, meaning your order is filled as soon as you pay for it.

Those are a few of the top reasons why electronic novels are displacing paperbacks for many an avid reader. As always, Ellora's Cave Publishing welcomes your questions and comments. We invite you to email us at service@ellorascave.com or write to us directly at: P.O. Box 787, Hudson, Ohio 44236-0787.

Printed in the United States
19826LVS00003B/1-57